The Pirate's Orphan

By Julia Inslee

Cover illustration by Rosemary Sack-Inslee

Published by Julia Inslee (jinslee14@gmail.com)
Copyright 2012
Coatesville, PA
ISBN # 978-1-105-71752-9
The Pirate's Orphan is available at lulu.com

Thank you to Mom for the years of editing, Dad for my first laptop, Ollie for the notecards, Rose for the artwork, and my wonderful community of extended family and friends, east, west, and overseas, for their unbelievable love and support throughout my life.

Prologue

The night was perfectly still; not a single cloud marred the illuminated sky as the brilliant moon shone like day on the cloaked figure approaching the convent door. One hand reached out from beneath her garment, grabbed the large brass knocker and broke the silence of the night with a crack. Her other hand remained hidden, guarding her sacred trust.

The large wooden door creaked open to reveal a kindly face, semi-obscured by a nun's habit.

"May I help you? It is late to be traveling," the kind face questioned with concern.

"Sister, I seek safe haven in the convent and to take orders," the cloaked figure responded with a hint of fatigue under her determined expression.

"This is not a decision to be entered upon lightly my child. You are welcome to a bed and a modest supper tonight, but wait until the morning to choose the cloistered life."

As if in response to this counsel, the bundle beneath the cloak began to wiggle and whimper, which grew into a cry, the cry of a hungry baby.

The sister peered at the cloak and then stared into the face under the hood with understanding. This wouldn't be the first time an unmarried woman had arrived with a child.

"She is hungry. We have traveled far. I seek a refuge for this child and myself. I have abandoned my life of sin for the sake of this child."

The resolve in the mysterious traveler's voice struck the sister, and the cry of the child in the still night drove pity into her heart. "Our door is always open to those who seek refuge. May I see the child?"

With this encouragement, the traveler delicately pushed back her cloak to reveal the wailing baby nestled in the crook of her arm. She raised the pitiable child to the outstretched hands of the sister, who took the refugee in her warm grasp. She coddled and cooed as she would have her own child, until it was soothed, its shining eyes staring up at her welcoming face with hope.

"You have shelter here darling for however long you seek it, *ma cherie*."

Chapter 1

Martinique 1738

The stark halls of the convent were quiet, as the inhabitants were still in morning vespers, all except Lucy, who made her way to the kitchen to prepare breakfast before the sisters entered the dining hall at seven o'clock sharp.

Lucy pulled eggs and ham out of the pantry and began beating and frying the ingredients. The Mother Superior had placed Lucy in charge of all kitchen preparations several years earlier, an attempt to quell her easy fall into boredom. She had lived in this convent on the French island of Martinique for as long as she could remember. The nuns were kind to her and had taught her French, English, sums, reading, and writing, a better education than most orphans could expect or most girls could hope for. Fortunately, Mother Superior had been adamant about her education, forcefully explaining that every girl should have the opportunity to grow a healthy mind. Lucy was grateful to have a home with so many aunts, mothers, and sisters, but there was always that nagging feeling, the same feeling that hit her now as she broke the eggs into a bowl to beat them—*I don't belong here.*

During the evenings, Lucy usually sat with Sister Regina and read adventure tales with her involving far off lands, duels, rapscallions, damsels in distress, and gallant saviors—these books were never approved of by the Mother Superior, so it was usually kept quiet. While reading about heroes and heroines with Sister, Lucy heard what little she knew about her parents. Sister Regina had been at the convent when the orphaned child arrived many years earlier. She was now in her late thirties but still had soft, delicate features. This kindly woman insisted on tormenting Lucy with the same vague details about her parentage again and again.

"Your mother left you in our care because she knew she couldn't give you a decent life." Sister Regina always began with the harsh truth; her mother had left her.

"But what was she like Sister?" Lucy pleaded each time.

"She was rumored to be a stubborn woman, who never backed down from a fight, especially if it concerned someone she loved."

"What about my father, Sister?"

"He was a seaman. He was revered for knowing his way around a ship." But that is all Sister would say.

Lucy was determined that one day she would find her parents and confront them as to why they had left her, but now wasn't the time. The nuns needed breakfast, so she shook off her nagging thoughts and finished arranging the tea on its tray.

Mother Superior entered the kitchen for her daily tete-a-tete with Lucy. "Good day Lucy. What do you have planned for us this morning?"

Lucy proudly showed the commanding matriarch of the convent a spread of scrambled eggs, baked ham, cheese, and toast she had carefully prepared.

"Looks lovely, as usual. You were the best thing to happen to this kitchen." Seeing a sheepish expression appear on Lucy's face, the astute Mother Superior continued, "But I think maybe you don't feel the same way."

Not wanting to seem unappreciative for all that she had at the convent, Lucy haltingly tried to explain. "Mother, I do like working here…and I thank you for the opportunity, but it's just that I'm not sure I am destined for a life in a kitchen."

Mother Superior pondered Lucy for a moment, "I don't doubt that. But remember, life is long and you never know where it might take you. Just be on the lookout for the next adventure." Mother patted Lucy on the shoulder and then made her way to the dining hall. Lucy watched her regal figure leave and returned to the task at hand.

***

After serving a much appreciated breakfast, Lucy went to the market by the port in Fort-de-France for provisions. The market was always a busy and bustling occasion, with fishermen hauling in fresh lobsters and conch from the bay and booth after booth of vendors yelling to prospective buyers about the deal of the day on local produce like breadfruit, yams, yucca, plantains, and sweet potatoes. Hundreds of people of all walks of life milled about looking at the specials of the day. Wealthy daughters of sugar plantation owners strolled the docks with the latest frilly and colorful fashions from Paris—hair piled high on their heads, parasols twirling in the hot sun, diligently followed by chaperons enlisted as sentries. Local village children ducking in and out of the crowds, causing glares from the more sedate and fashionable, added to the helter-skelter atmosphere. Household slaves purposefully went from salesman to salesman purchasing fish and vegetables for the families of others.

Amongst this milieu, Lucy was inspecting the day's lobster catch, when a disturbance in the crowd caught her attention.

"Look wha ya've done ya stupid darkie."

The crowds, intrigued by this vulgar outburst resonating throughout the market, began to gather. Lucy moved closer to see a shabbily dressed, bearded sailor looking down on a pretty, young slave woman who kneeled at his feet with her head down. She mumbled repeatedly, "*J'suis désolée, monsieur.*" A basket of fish lay in disarray on the ruffian's boots.

"What are ya babblin'? Ya stupid clumsy cow. Ya've ruined me best shoes," the sailor yelled. He bent down and picked up one of the slimy dead fish and then violently struck the girl across the face. The scaly weapon landed with a thwack, and the girl cried out in shock, slumping to the ground. The man raised his arm, wielding the fish again, readying to strike the poor girl. At that moment, a large, orange yam struck the assailant on the side of the head. "Wha the bloody devil?" he screamed out in pain.

The crowd turned in surprise at this new action in the unveiling drama. Lucy stepped out with fierce determination in her glare as she stared the man square in the eyes; actually eye, for she noticed as he turned to face her that his left eye wasn't there at all, but sewn shut, with a deep scar extending from his forehead to his lip. The ghastly sight made her step back in alarm, but the anger in the man's voice brought her back to her present plight.

"Ya dare throw a potato at me bitch? I can beat ya just the same as the darkie."

"You will beat neither me nor this girl. Before you lay a hand on either one of us, another yam shall crack you in the head; I'm thinking right between the eyes." With this latest threat, Lucy pulled out yet another orb in preparation for the fight. As her hand came out of the basket, the sailor's eye grew large, as if he saw some horror. He stared, dumbstruck at Lucy's hand.

"Where'd ya get that ring, gurl?" he questioned in disbelief. A tremor had entered his voice. Even the crowd and the girl at his feet noticed the remarkable difference in this tyrant. Seeing that the fight seemed to be over, the crowd began to disperse, and the hunched girl took the opportunity of her attacker's distraction to flee the scene. She quickly disappeared into the bustle.

Lucy looked down at the gold ring on her right hand before she responded with, "It was my mother's ring. If you plan on robbing me of it, I suggest you change your mind. You will regret it." She raised the yam yet again to prove her seriousness.

The ring was very unusual, as it was engraved with the letter "*A*" on the front. Two sabers crossed blades, making up the sides of the "*A.*" Engraved on the inside of the ring were the words *Always My Bonny - R.* Sister Regina had given it to Lucy on her sixteenth birthday, the only object left to her by her errant mother. It wasn't pretty, but it was precious to the orphan. It gave Lucy the only clue to the identities of her parents. Her mother could have been an Alice or an Aster. Her father might have been Richard or Reginald. Maybe the sabers meant her father was a captain in the navy? And maybe her mother waited day after day for him to return home to her, but he never did—he was lost to the sea like many a noble seaman. And when he didn't return, her mother was left destitute and couldn't afford to keep her baby. At least that was one of her theories.

"Yur mother ya say?" At this information the bearded man gazed at the chocolate brown eyes and the locks of dark auburn hair that fell in waves over the girl's shoulders. He noticed the shape and the fierce look in the eyes. There was a certain familiarity about her. And he had heard rumors that *that* woman had escaped with her baby. *Yes, it really could be 'er daughter*, he thought to himself. *That whore.* With hatred burning in his voice he growled, "Aye, if that be yur mother, may she burn in 'ell for the misery she caused, and may ya suffer for bein' the brat of an ungrateful whore."

Lucy stepped back, anger rising up from her stomach, but also curiosity.

"How dare you speak of her in that way. I don't believe a filthy vermin like you could have known my mother."

"I knew yur mother very well. I was married to 'er."

At these shocking words Lucy's arm fell limply to her side, the yam dropped from her hand, and her mind went blank. It couldn't be. This awful man couldn't be her father. She half whispered the next question. "Are you my father then?"

From his cruel lips burst an appalling cackle. "Yur a bastard spawn. Me, yur father? Ha! I'd sooner be father to a darkie. The only thing that bitch gave me was this scar." He pointed to the empty eye socket flanked by the red gash. "She were a cruel and 'eartless slut. Best day of me life was the day she disappeared." He spat these words out with such contempt and malice that Lucy wanted to run, but she had one final question that needed asking.

"What was her name?"

The creature before her stood motionless for what seemed like an eternity, a grin spreading over his cruel face. "I nev'r thought I'd say the name agen. Anne Bonny." And with that, Bonny turned and disappeared into the crowd, leaving Lucy to stare at the spot where he'd just fled from. The most repulsive human she'd ever met had just given her the first real kernel of information about her mother.

Chapter 2

Lucy's head swam in confusion as she darted down the halls of the convent; the echo of her heels reverberating off the walls was nearly as loud as the voices in her head.

That disgusting person couldn't have been familiar with my mother, let alone been her husband. It's impossible. But he knew her name; if her name really was Anne Bonny. But it must have been her name. Anne Bonny— it matches the "A" on my ring. And the inscription calls her "My Bonny."

The horrible slurs this stranger had aimed at a mother Lucy had never met stirred a hatred in her blood that she had never felt before in her sheltered life. Only mercenaries from her novels could speak such filth about a lady. *Or could it be true? Maybe she was as he said and that's why she gave me up…? No, I can't believe it.*

Lucy's one sane thought was to spill the morning's events to Sister Regina. She arrived at the Sister's chamber door; she burst through, startling the woman on the other side of the door from her reading. Sister Regina looked up with a jolt as the wild-eyed girl flew into her room. "*Ma cherie. Qu'est que c'est?* You look awful."

Lucy launched into the thoughts that troubled her. "At the market…this disgusting man said he …knew…that he was married to my mother. He said her name was Anne Bonny. He described her with such foul words and said she was cruel." During the rant that poured forth from Lucy, she paced frantically back and forth across the room. She stopped abruptly at the gasp that escaped from Sister Regina. Lucy looked up and saw horror spread across her face. At this, Lucy ran and knelt down beside the distraught Sister.

"How did I frighten you Sister? I'm sorry."

With her lips barely moving, the name slipped out, "James Bonny."

"Sister, how do you know this man?"

"Could it be? I thought he would be long dead." Sister shifted her gaze down to Lucy. "How did he know you?"

"He recognized my ring. Please Sister. How do you know this man? You never even gave me the name of my mother, but you know her husband?" Anxiety was growing in Lucy's voice.

"Lucy, there are things that have been kept from you. Things I promised not to tell you to protect you." Sister's voice was calm, but her eyes spoke of painful memories. Sadness was hidden there.

"All the nights I asked you questions about my parents, pleading with you at least for a name and you told me nothing." Lucy now spoke in a flat, dead tone. "I demand you tell me who this man is."

"I will tell you what I know of Bonny, but no more than that." At Lucy's attempt to protest, Sister Regina cut her off. "That is all you will get from me now."

Chapter 3

The Carolinas 1700-1717

Anne Bonny was born in County Cork, Ireland, the illegitimate child of a prominent lawyer and his cook and mistress. When the news of this scandal broke in the local area, the shamed couple was forced to leave; Richard Cormac's understandably enraged wife had threatened to have his mistress imprisoned for the indiscretion.

With his savings, Cormac was able to leave Ireland and embark on a journey with his new family to the Carolinas in the American colonies. The voyage was long and difficult. Sickness broke out on more than one occasion, which, coupled with the cramped quarters below deck, created an unbearably foul stench. For the last two months of the voyage, passengers subsisted only on dried pork for all meals and a spare amount of water.

Upon arriving in the Carolinas, Cormac was able to purchase a large tract of land and begin extracting resin from the pine trees to manufacture tar for the British navy, which proved profitable for the Irishman, and his wife and daughter lived a comfortable life because of it.

Time passed and Anne grew into a young woman—some older women in the area would have said she was growing into a wild young woman with no propriety. Anne was often seen riding her gray mare at a full gallop, her red locks streaming behind her, and her skirt hiked up to her thighs. As rumors of her behavior spread, Anne's grin grew wider, accentuating the sparkle in her dark brown eyes. By the age of sixteen, Anne was known for picking fights with the local boys if they merely looked at her the wrong way.

"Hey Annie, looks like you've been rolling around in the barn; is it with the pigs, because it's definitely not with a man," they'd taunt her as she entered the general store with smears of dirt on her bodice and her hair standing up wildly.

"From the boys I've seen in this town, I think I'd prefer the company of pigs," she replied and then continued her shopping. Later she saw young Robby walking to the river as she was riding. She pulled her riding crop out, and as she flew past, wrapped him on the back of the head ruthlessly yelling, "Since you act like a pig, you'll be beaten as a pig."

***

During the summer of 1717 Anne's father hired a new plantation manager, a fellow Irishman by the name of James

Bonny. Bonny was a swarthy fellow who had spent years as a
sailor before settling for a life on land. He was the proud owner of
a smooth tongue, which he had used to full advantage to woo many
a girl from Ireland to the Carolinas. Anne was instantly struck by
the appearance of this worldly and rugged farm hand and made a
point of taking her rides past the fields where Bonny was working
during the day.

"Mr. Bonny, I thought you might like a dram of whiskey on
this hot day."

"Miss Cormac, yur most kind. Whiskey just 'appens to be
me favorite way to forget the 'eat. Yur lookin' mighty fair up
there on that fine mare."

"We understand each other, Fire and me. She's my oldest
friend."

"One with yur eyes should have more friends than just a
'orse. I'm sure there be many a lad who yu've broken."

"If by broken you mean beaten, then yes."

"I've been told yur a wild one. I bet they deserved it."

"They did, and more."

Bonny and Anne began meeting in the woods, in the barn,
down by the river, or anywhere else that provided cover from the
eyes of her father. Cormac had it in his mind that Anne would
marry a wealthy landowner, or maybe a merchant, someone who
could care for her financially and keep her in the quality of

19

lifestyle that he felt she deserved. Anne had no interest in this plan, as the merchants and landowners she had seen were all either old as Methuselah or soul crushingly boring. A man who worked with his hands to earn his way and traveled the world's oceans was a more appealing prospect.

One afternoon, Cormac entered the barn to catch his horse up to ride to town; instead, he came upon Bonny stroking the hair from Anne's face, her hands on his waist and a flush in both their cheeks.

"How dare you look upon my daughter or touch her with your rough hands. Anne, you are meant for a better man. You know not what you're doing my girl. Bonny, I never want to see you anywhere near my land again," Cormac thundered, his face growing redder and his fists balling at his sides. "Get out; get out before I whip you all the way to the gate, you dog!"

"Father, if James goes then so do I; I promise you that. These pretty dandies that you plan to marry me off to be of no interest to me. You are blind if you think otherwise. You will not choose a husband for me father, and I will not be kept from James."

Just as she had promised, even though she'd been forcefully thrown in her room and Bonny had been run off the plantation by the local authorities, Anne plotted her escape that very night. She stole quietly out of her room into the darkened shadows of the sleeping house and made her way down to her father's office. Rifling through his desk drawers she came upon her father's stash of bills. As she pocketed the sum, the door creaked open to reveal a young, freckle-faced house servant. Henny spoke with the lilting, singsong German accent of a girl still relatively fresh to the Americas. "Mizz Anne, vat iz happenink here? Vhy are you avake, in ze master'z shtudy?"

"Get out of here Henny."

"You are shtealink from de master? He'z goink to blame me if he finkz any of hiz money iz gone." Henny turned and was about to cry out and wake the house to the mischief, for she wasn't about to waste the two years she had spent as an indentured servant to the Cormacs on the stupidity of a spoiled girl.

However, Anne wasn't about to let her plans be deterred and her freedom curtailed by the skittishness of a servant, so before Henny screamed a word, Anne struck her over the head with a candlestick, which she had hastily snatched from the desk in desperation. Henny fell to the floor with a thump, blood pooling around her body from the gash in her head. At the sight of the expanding blood and the suddenly lifeless form at her feet, a panic began to grow in Anne's belly, for Anne had only meant to keep the girl quiet, not strike her down.

"Oh Henny, you shouldn't have come in here. You would have spoiled it all. I'm sorry, I'm sorry," she cried to the fallen woman.

Knowing she couldn't linger, Anne collected her thoughts and refocused on her goal. She found her father's money, and with the tears still brimming in her eyes, she fled from the house she had grown up in and the family that had cared for her.

Anne met Bonny on the outskirts of the plantation, and the duo made their escape to the port of Charles Towne, where they married and then boarded a ship destined for the island of New Providence in the Bahamas.

Chapter 4

New Providence 1717

In that time, the Bahamian Islands, and most especially New Providence, were a wild haven for lowlifes and debauchery, mostly inhabited by soldiers, merchants, prostitutes, and pirates. The docks were bustling with ships coming in, sailors unloading supplies, and merchants wheeling and dealing for the best profits. Slave ships entered the port with the wails of their human cargo, followed by auctions attended by plantation owners in search of free labor. Sailors on leave after months at sea took advantage of the abundant women and rum found in the watering holes that littered the port area. Scruffy sailors enjoying the local entertainment could be seen reeling around the streets, picking fights, and singing until they passed out in the gutters.

Anne Bonny and her husband arrived in this colorful port town in the fall of 1717. With the money Anne had lifted from her father's desk the couple was able to take lodgings above the infamous Rooster's Crow saloon. The rooms were shabby but bearable, especially for the newlyweds.

For a short time, Anne and Bonny were content. Anne cooked and minded the apartment, and Bonny greeted her with a peck or two on the cheek when he returned from a day of looking for work along the docks. But with the proximity to the pub, Bonny took to frequenting the establishment, mixing with the smarmier dregs of society, and drinking into the wee hours. He became quite content to live off his wife's money.

"James, our money is running out. We have enough until the end of the month and then we'll be out on the streets, begging for your liquor." As time wore on, Anne became increasingly irritated with the drunken lout that spent his days sleeping in their room and spent his nights carousing. Bonny's charm was beginning to wear off.

"Woman, I'm gittin' settled. Makin' contacts with businessmen. Jus' last night a feller offered me an important position in the col'ny. Yu'll see. I'll make us rich."

"While you've been making these so called contacts, I've been cleaning up after you and scrimping to keep us fed. But with you drinking away my savings, it's barely enough to keep food on the table."

***

The proprietor of this fine drinking establishment was a man of a mere twenty-three years of age who called himself Lafitte. With his eye for the gentlemen, he made an unusual

24

landlord for a notorious watering hole for female-starved sailors, but because he guarded over the ladies of the night like his own sisters, the sought after women frequented his establishment more than others.

Pierre Lafitte was born in France to a pair of traveling theater performers, but when he was nine years of age his mother died while giving birth to his sister. The grieved father moved his young son and daughter to New Providence to begin a new life as an innkeeper, a profession in which his flair for the theatrical would serve him well. He enjoyed seven prosperous years in New Providence, until he was cut down in a bar room brawl, leaving Lafitte to manage the Rooster's Crow and care for his young sister, both of which he took to with determination and passion.

Lafitte had inherited his father's jolly nature and quickly became a renowned lover of storytelling and gossip, a trait essential to a publican. The transient sailors could always count on a thirst quenching pint and the latest news from Lafitte. But the news from Lafitte's lips was usually a bit more exciting than the truth—a flare or two added for flavor.

Shortly after Anne took residence above the Rooster's Crow, Lafitte began recounting a tale that became a favorite with his clientele. "This girl runs away from her fancy plantation where she was fanned and fed ripe strawberries by servant boys. She was betrothed to a handsome young landowner, who was so rich that he

25

could shower gold coins on the children when he rode into town. But for one flaw he would have been a perfect husband— his shark was the size of a shrimp."

At this point the guffaws of Lafitte's rapt audience exploded into the silence like a thunderclap. Sparked with interest at the festivities below her rooms, Anne wandered downstairs to find this handsome thespian with his well-coiffed, black hair, olive skin, and light blue eyes (which stood in stark contrast to his otherwise dark features) gesticulating wildly in emphasis to each new sordid detail.

Lafitte continued with his tale in ignorance of his new audience. "Along comes a farmhand, with muscles that bulged in all the right places. As she watched him wield an axe to chop the firewood, she took a fancy to him. 'Oh, kind sir, I've brought you a glass of lemonade. You must be so hot from your exertions.' 'Aye, lassie I am,' the strapping lad replied with a gleam in his eye. And with that he ripped off her bodice and took her for a good roll in the hay. 'Kind sir, you're a python.'" The audience howled again. "The father of this harlot discovers the lovers and beats them both mercilessly as he would his horse, but the girl cared not. At dusk, she stole all the money in her father's house and eloped with the farmhand, and now she lives in poverty here in New Providence, all for a snake."

"The poverty we live in is the filthy establishment that you keep, knave. Only a worm would be jealous of a snake's good fortune." Anne approached the storyteller, a glint in her eye, forcing the crowd to separate.

"Fine lady doth have issues with our humble home?"

"No, I have issues with exaggeration, sir. The fortunate farmhand of which you speak is less of a python, and more of a turd."

With this, the crowd and the excellent proprietor let loose a raucous guffaw.

"You are welcome to a drink my lady."

***

Anne and Lafitte became fast friends from that moment on, Lafitte offering work washing dishes and scrubbing the bar clean. Anne spoke of her life in the Carolinas, while Lafitte regaled her with the scoop on his clientele.

"Your fine husband has taken to informing for the crown."

"What could that lout possibly know that would be of any interest to anyone?"

"You'd be surprised, *ma Cherie Rouge*. During the course of Bonny's excessive drinking he has become friendly with certain nefarious elements of the sea." Lafitte looked at Anne knowingly.

"You mean pirates?"

27

Lafitte nodded. "These independent businessmen have loose tongues after quenching their thirsts. Bonny gleans what he can and takes it to the attention of the Governor. Have you noticed the absence of some of our more colorful clientele, like Devilish Dave, Ronald Bulwark, and Pete Spark?"

"Indeed yes. Devilish Dave left pretty good tips."

"The Governor is cleaning up the colony. With Bonny's information, these men often end up with their necks in a noose. Bonny's betraying dangerous men."

"Well, I hope they kill him, then I'll be free of that mistake," Anne stated unsympathetically.

Chapter 5

Martinique 1738

"That's who James Bonny is, a drunken, lazy, lout." Sister Regina sat quietly with her hands folded in her lap after finishing her story.

"Sister, what happened to my mother in New Providence?" Lucy pleaded. "So Anne must have been my mother. We share the same surname." Lucy was visibly excited. Between the ring and the name Cormac, she had enough proof that Anne really was her mother.

"I know you want to believe that you've figured out who your mother is, but you aren't on the right path, *ma petite*."

Lucy desperately clung to what she knew was true. "I don't believe you anymore Sister. You don't want me to find my mother, so I can't trust you for the truth about her."

"Beyond what I've told you, I would be betraying a confidence." As she said this, Sister Regina felt cold inside. She was keeping so much from this child whom she had nurtured and loved from before she could walk. She felt she was doing more

29

harm than good, but it hadn't been her decision to hide the truth from Lucy.

Attempting to change the drift of the conversation, Sister murmured, "I don't want to remember the life that came before; I've tried to find peace here in the convent. I'm still haunted in my dreams by the past, but during the waking hours I turn my thoughts to God to push those memories away."

There was no turning back though. "You say you won't betray a confidence, but you're betraying me by keeping this information from me." Hot, bitter tears dripped from Lucy's eyes.

Sister Regina placed her hand on Lucy's head, stroking her hair. "I've made promises."

"No, you've betrayed me, and I will not forgive you for that Sister." Lucy pushed Sister's hand away and jumped up, fleeing from the room and slamming the thick door behind her. Sister Regina watched helplessly as Lucy disappeared. Emotion poured out of her for the child she'd nursed through sickness and taught to cook. She buried her face in her delicate hands, trying, but failing to push back the dark images that flooded her mind. *"Pardonne-moi, ma fille,"* she cried aloud to the emptiness.

***

One thought filled Lucy's head as she ran to her room, *I will find my mother. Sister said this Anne Bonny landed in New*

Providence.   Maybe the answers I want can be found there? She might still live there.

She headed to the kitchen, but instead of preparing dinner like she had done every day for the last two years at this time, she grabbed some bread and cheese.   Lucy returned to her room and quickly gathered a few clothes and bundled them into a sack along with the bits of food.   With the words of Mother Superior still ringing in her ears, *"Be on the lookout for the next adventure,"* Lucy slipped out of the convent towards the docks for the second time that day.

Chapter 6

The *Queen Mary* was docked in the harbor of Fort-de-France early the next morning. The crew was loading it with rum and sugar to be sold in the city of Philadelphia after a stop on the island of New Providence. Several passengers were also making their way on board.

Lucy waited and watched unseen from a safe distance until the correct moment presented itself. And eventually it did present itself, in the form of a rather frazzled looking, but well-dressed woman, who was desperately trying to keep in line a passel of eight children—big ones, little ones, and everything in between. With one small, aggressive girl poking another whining boy, one frilly pink young woman yelling at a much younger girl with yellow curls to stay away from the edge of the dock, and three identical, short, rotund boys chasing some very frightened birds, chaos seemed to exude from the family.

Lucy quickly slipped into step with the girl that looked to be the eldest in this clan—the pink one—and began to chat with her new best friend. "On your way to New Providence too? We must get to know each other if we are going to be stuck on a ship for days together. What takes you on this voyage?"

Without even batting an eye, the girl replied, "Our uncle lives in New Providence. He's a merchant and wants to take two of my brothers on as apprentices. And where they go, we all go."

"There sure are a lot of you. Your mother looks a bit tired," Lucy noticed.

"She's looked that way since the triplets were two months old."

The tribe, after much cajoling and rebuke, finally managed to reach the gangplank. A sailor greeted the matriarch with a nod. "Hello madam. It's a fine day to be at sea. There should be no problems. Are these little 'uns all with you?" he asked while eyeing the rum lot.

The mother smiled faintly. "Yes, all with me. I hope they will be no trouble on the voyage."

"If they are, we just throw them overboard," the sailor joked. The mother quickly ushered her children past the insensitive sailor.

Lucy continued a pleasant conversation with the eldest daughter, who was overjoyed to have another girl to talk to about parasols and the best colors in dresses. Lucy feigned interest in these topics, staying close to her new friend's elbow, until they had all boarded. Through an extensive exchange of pleasantries, Lucy learned the girl's name was Celia Bertrand. Her father was of some importance in the French government, and was thus in France, so Celia and the rest of the clan were going to stay with her mother's relations on New Providence.

With some effort, Lucy extricated herself from her vociferous friend, promising they would reunite at a later time, and looked for a safe hideaway far from the eyes of the crew.

***

Deep within the hull of the ship, Lucy hid herself in the dank, dark, behind large barrels, which reeked of rum. Rats squirmed at her feet. The steady sway of the ship, mingled with the rank smells that permeated the dark, all worked to tie her stomach in knots. On top of Lucy's nasal and stomach ailments, fear and anger continued to do battle in her head. Lucy had never spent a night away from the convent in her entire life, and now she was stealing away into the unknown while infuriated with the mysteries of her parentage. It was both hurtful and aggravating that the woman who had been her most trusted friend and confidante would purposefully hide the truth from her. *What could be so bad about the past and my parents to cause such secrecy?*

But even with these distractions battling in her head, another sound caught her interest. Something in the dark had fallen to the floor of the ship with a plunk. Lucy was loathe to reveal her own presence on the ship but was too agitated to sit still without knowing what else might be hiding in the dark with her.

"Hello. Is anybody there?" she whispered.

There was no sound in response, just the constant lapping of waves. Most likely a rat had knocked something over.

Lucy got up from her hiding spot and walked quietly towards the place where the sound had emanated from just a moment ago. Lucy pushed aside a crate labeled "SUGAR" to find a pair of eyes and a dagger pointing at her; that was all she could see through the thin streams of light. Not a rat.

"*Bouge pas*," the voice commanded in French.

"*Calmez vous*," Lucy responded and stepped back cautiously. "If you're worried I'll report you as a stowaway, don't. I too am a stowaway," she explained, her voice attempting to remain calm.

The bearer of the knife spoke back from the dark. "I will kill you if you come closer."

"I'll go back to my hiding place and not bother you. I just heard a noise and wanted to know what it was. I won't bother you anymore." Lucy began to move backwards and stepped into a patch of light.

"Wait, stop," the voice ordered. Lucy froze, her face highlighted in a band of sunlight that streamed in through a crack in the side of the ship.

"You are the lady from yesterday morning at the dock. You threw the yam." The voice had changed, softened.

"Yes, that was me. You were there in the market?"

In response to this question, the knife and the glowing eyes moved forward from the darkness until fragments of light illuminated the figure of a young girl with ebony skin, the dagger still poised for action.

"You were the girl who spilled the fish." Recognition dawned on Lucy. "What are you doing here?"

"Same as you most likely, running away."

"But how did you get away?"

"That's none of your business."

"No, you're right. We each have our secrets. I won't turn you in, I promise. Can you please put the knife away?"

The knife cautiously withdrew to the girl's side.

"Well, that's a little better. My name is Lucy, Lucy Cormac."

The girl just stared.

"You can tell me your name. Here, look, I have some bread. I grabbed it before I left home." Lucy dug into the sack she had hastily packed with necessities and pulled out a chunk of bread. She thrust it towards the girl, entreating her to take the meager snack.

"It's Gracie, thank you." Gracie took the bread, happier than she would admit to being offered bread. She hadn't eaten anything in hours.

The two girls bit into their dinners and relaxed into the darkness, preparing for many hours of being cooped up in the dank abyss of the hull. It was a comfort to both of the runaways to share the dark. The hull didn't seem as frightening, and the journey became more bearable, at least until this new found security vanished.

Chapter 7

After several hours of sitting in near silence, an ear splitting blast broke the monotony below deck. Screaming, shouting, and scrambling above deck quickly followed. The pounding of heavy feet and the shouts of, "Grab your weapons!" "All hands to deck!" "We're under attack!" brought a new panic to the stowaways.

"*Mon Dieu,* we're trapped down here." Lucy crossed herself out of habit. "What do we do now?"

"Most likely we die now," Gracie dryly replied.

"No we won't. I refuse to die now. We can't just stay here in the open though. Move. Behind these boxes. Now!" Lucy grabbed the other girl's hand, ignoring the knife still tightly clasped in Gracie's fingers. Lucy pulled the weight behind her until they were wedged deep within the hull, safely hidden behind crates filled with sugar.

"Maybe if we pray we will escape unmolested," Lucy said to alleviate their fears. But the sound of the clashing of metal and the crack of pistols firing did not make this hope seem probable.

"Somehow I don't think praying is the solution to this problem," Gracie deadpanned.

The two women sat and waited in the dark, listening to the battle above. Lucy could hear her heart pounding violently in her chest. And then, as quickly as it had begun, the scuffle was over. A shout of victory could be heard from above.

The thud of the trap door to the hull opening brought light into the dark recesses of the ship. Emerging through the stream of light on the hull's steps Lucy saw two black boots leading a pair of knee-high black trousers, a slim waist tied with a bright red sash, a tall lanky body draped in a white linen shirt, and a scruffy, but handsome face, framed in shoulder- length, dirty, blond curls, topped with a tri-cornered hat.

"Ahoy, Silas and Seamus, we got us a good load down here. Looks like sugar and, praise the lord, rum," the intruder gloated. With these words, two more men in the same vane as the first stomped down the steps; however, they looked older and more weathered in their features, one even bearing a nasty scar down his forearm.

"Seamus, I told you it would have rum. You owe me forty-seven pints," the one with the scar boasted.

"And I told you there'd be sugar, so you owe me fifty-six pints," the one called Seamus replied.

"Yes, but you said there wouldn't be any rum because it had come from Martinique and their supply has been low this year, due to recent storms," the other, presumably Silas, retaliated.

"No, I said the likelihood of there being sugar on board was far greater due to the upsurge in slave labor on the island in recent months."

"Both of you old fools, quit bickering and pick up the crates," the younger man cut them off in exasperation. "If given the chance you two would argue if the sun is out today."

Silas started, "Technically there is a light cloud cover masking the full strength of the sun."

"Shh, pick up the crate or we'll never get off this ship, and the navy will get here and cut your tongues out," the young one silenced the jabberer.

Each of the two older intruders hefted a crate onto his shoulder and labored towards the light in the hatch.

As they disappeared, Seamus picked up where they'd left off, "The clouds were only covering the sun this morning, but at this moment we have full sun…," the jabbering faded.

Meanwhile, the third man was still perusing the spoils in the semi-darkness. He began to move forward, towards the spot where two women were crouched, awaiting their inevitable discovery.

Lucy's mind turned to the books she'd read with Sister Regina for all those years. *Pirates! These men had to be pirates*, she thought. True fear was taking over her body, tensing every muscle as she saw the figure looming closer. She had read too many tales of these rogues of the sea to not know what would happen if she was discovered, either death by gruesome means, or worse, an attack on her virtue. These two scenarios alternated in her head, growing more terrifying and vivid each second. *If I'm going to be murdered, I'll do it on my own terms.* Determined, she grabbed for the dagger still clenched in the hands of her companion. She whispered to Gracie, "Don't move," and sprang out from behind the boxes.

In a clear, firm voice she addressed the pirate. "Do not step one inch closer or I will slice you from your nose to your nave." This was a threat pirates often used that Lucy thought especially menacing from her books.

The recipient of this animosity had become a statue at the sudden appearance of a crazed, knife-wielding woman. His deep blue eyes, at first concentrated on the point of the knife, roamed up the bodice, to the wild, dark eyes, and finally to the loose red-tinged, dark hair of the woman who was now verbally threatening him.

"Do not tempt me to use this sir. You will not do harm to me; I swear to you."

Finally, the pirate was able to find his words. "Miss, I do not wish you any harm. We are here solely for supplies for our crew. And I think you mean naval."

"What?"

"The saying is: I'll slit you from nose to naval."

Lucy brushed off her momentary fluster at being corrected by a pirate. "I don't trust your intentions. I know what you are."

"You are wise to not trust the intentions of strange men, but you have my word of honor that you will not be harmed." He said this with such sincerity, and the expression on his face spoke truth. Lucy began to hope for the best; nonetheless, she did not lower the knife.

"I won't be lowering this dagger, and I will only take you at your word when I am left in peace."

"That is your right. If you allow me to borrow some of this sugar, I will be on my way and will the sooner leave you in peace," the pirate smirked at her, mildly amused by his present circumstance.

"Then carry on with your borrowing," Lucy gave permission to her captive.

At this moment, the sounds of Silas and Seamus's constant bickering grew louder as they returned for their next loads of loot. The one called Silas, who was slightly shorter and balder than the other one, noticed the scene in front of him first, focusing on the knife pointing at his captain. He abruptly broke off his argument extolling the value of chamomile in curing sea sickness over ginger root and pulled his pistol from his belt, deftly aiming it at the young woman.

"I will shoot before you plunge that knife. If you value your life, put down the knife," Silas commanded.

"Silas, lower your pistol. This young lady and I have reached an agreement. We take what we want and leave her with her virtue intact, then I leave unscathed," the captive explained to his loyal crewman.

"Captain, are you sure? She looks as though she'd run you through just as soon as look at you," Seamus wryly commented.

"Aye, she does, but if I wandered upon myself whilst hidden in the dark, I'd want to kill me too. But I am sure she will do no harm, if I do none," reasoned the captain.

"Captain?" Lucy questioned.

"Yes, my lady, you have captured a pirate captain. Captain Sebastian Strongbow at your service," he joked gallantly.

Silas slowly put away his firearm. "Now gather those two crates there; they contain powder," Sebastian ordered his rescuers. We need to get off this vessel. We've taken too long as is. If you'll excuse me miss, I'd like to borrow this sack of sweet potatoes." Sebastian grinned and then reached down at Lucy's feet and picked up the large bulging brown sack. Lucy followed his every move with her eyes, relaxing a bit, but staying on the alert for any threatening motion.

Silas and Seamus each grabbed a crate labeled "POWDER" and headed toward the stairs, passing by Lucy. Lucy's ring glinted briefly in the light, catching Seamus's eye. His face fell and so did his loot, which thudded to the ground and cracked open, spilling out the black, granule contents of the box.

Silas yelled, "Seamus, you could have blown us all up, you klutz." But Seamus didn't even hear. He was staring at the ring with glistening eyes. His voice cracked as he asked, "Where did you get that ring?"

"It was my mother's, Anne Bonny. Do you recognize it?"

"Silas, is it possible?"

Silas approached with curiosity. Upon seeing the ring and hearing that familiar and dear name, he looked upon the face of the girl with interest and sadness. "I don't believe it. Can it be the bairn all grown up? That's most assuredly Anne Bonny's ring."

Seamus chimed in. "Anne disappeared so long ago with a wee babe." His voice faded and trembled with these last words as he tried to forget the past. "What is your name my dear?"

"I am Lucy Cormac. I must have been that baby." Lucy's throat clenched. "I've never known my mother, but I left my home in the convent in Fort-de-France to find her. You knew Anne? Do you know where I can find her?" Hope sprang up from deep within Lucy. These marauders had actually known her mother. It crossed Lucy's mind that it seemed Anne was only acquainted with dangerous men. She'd have to ponder that at a later time. At the present it didn't matter who could lead her to Anne, and this odd duo might know where to locate her.

But that hope was quickly dampened when Silas answered, "We have no idea where Anne is now. She literally disappeared."

"But, there is one man who might have a clue," Seamus added.

"Who? Tell me please," Lucy pleaded.

"Seamus, no. We can't. You know we can't," Silas pleaded with his friend.

Seamus ignored Silas's entreaty. "His name is Pierre Lafitte. He was a good friend to Anne. If anyone might know where to find her, it would be him."

"The man who owns the Rooster's Crow?" Lucy clarified, remembering the name from Sister Regina's story.

Seamus nodded. He turned back to his friend, "She has a right Silas. Seventeen years have passed, and it is time to accept the truth of the past. This girl…and us." Seamus's voice trailed off.

"You must take me to him. Please, I beg you," Lucy pleaded.

Sebastian, throughout this odd exchange between his crew and this strange girl, had stood and listened silently, but now he broke in. "We cannot take you with us. It's too dangerous. A pirate ship is no place for a woman. We are not a passenger ship."

"I can take care of myself. I do not fear discomfort. I can and will suffer through any difficulty with the hope of finding my mother at the end."

Silas added, "Captain, she seems ready to handle herself." He hesitated before adding quietly, "It's in her blood. Your mother was one of the best pirates I ever met."

Silence and shock greeted this revelation.

"How? No…That's not possible….It can't be…" Lucy stammered.'

Suddenly, the group below decks could hear a shift in mood from above. Cheers rang out from the crew of the *Queen Mary*, and the cry of fear and chaos burst from the pirates. "Captain Strongbow, a naval ship has been spotted off the starboard. We need to leave, now," a voice shouted down the hatch frantically.

"Lads we're done here. Flee now! We bid you adieu Miss," Sebastian ordered.

"I'm coming with you, with or without your permission," Lucy countered.

"I'll vouch for her sir," Seamus spoke up.

"Fine, I take no responsibility for you or your comfort."

"And my lady's maid is coming as well." Lucy turned towards Gracie's hiding place. "Gracie, it's okay. You can come out now." From behind the boxes, Gracie slipped out.

At the appearance of a second woman, Sebastian rolled his eyes. "Oh bloody hell."

Chapter 8

The two women were greeted by stares and wonder, and then hoots and lewd comments, by the crew of ragtag ruffians who'd been at sea without women for several months. But the crew didn't have much time for ogling and distraction before Captain Strongbow gave orders to pull anchor and get under way. There was no time for hesitation, even if that hesitation was caused by a pretty face and tight bodice. A British naval ship was now in sight off the starboard bow, approaching rapidly. The crew worked smoothly and efficiently, hauling in the anchor and letting fly the main sail. And with the wind in their favor, the sail caught, and the ship sped happily over the white crested sea.

Lucy was anxious to talk further with Silas and Seamus but had to settle for some time later, after the ship was safely distanced from the British naval ship. To distract herself, Lucy turned her attention to the problem of Gracie, who had followed her onto the *Peril* without a single word. She stood frozen at the rail of the ship, oblivious to the chaos around her, staring out to the horizon. Lucy approached carefully. *"Comment vas-tu*, Gracie?"

At this seemingly absurd question, Gracie began to giggle. "How am I? Today I ran away from my home, stole away on a ship, and have been attacked and captured by pirates. I think it's going pretty well, don't you?"

"At least you have a sense of humor about it," remarked Lucy, somewhat hurt at Gracie's sarcastic manner.

"No, what I have is nothing to lose. You know, today was the first day that I made a personal choice, the choice to run away. But by following you, I seem to be back where I started, without freedom of choice."

Being slightly upset at this accusation Lucy fired back, "Well why did you follow me? I was only trying to help you. You would have been caught on that ship at some point anyway, and then you would have just been sent back to the plantation and probably punished. And I don't believe these men have ill intentions towards us. You could have made the personal choice to stay on the *Queen Mary*. No one forced you to follow me."

Gracie listened and waited for a pause in Lucy's rant. "You threw the yam."

"What?" Lucy's expression changed from frustration to confusion.

"At the market that morning, you threw the yam at that disgusting creature. It was in that moment that I swore I would never cower again. I would never let anyone make me feel worthless again. I would throw the yam next time. So by following you, I figured I could protect you, especially since you decided to run off with a crew of pirates; you might need some protection. Since you came to my rescue, I owe you a good turn." Gracie trailed off and then turned her gaze back out to sea.

"If you plan on playing hero, I'm glad you have a knife and not a yam at the moment; it might prove more useful."

And with that, Lucy left Gracie to contemplate. Lucy had spied Seamus winding through the working sailors and went to pick his brain.

"Here lass, I brought you stew from below. I thought you might be a might peckish after today's excitements." Seamus held out the bowl to Lucy.

"I am a bit hungry. I haven't eaten since…maybe that was yesterday that I had my last good meal." She actually couldn't remember the last time she had eaten anything besides a hunk of bread. So much had happened recently. It must have been yesterday that she met Bonny at the wharf. Lucy took the stew offered to her and slurped it down. It was surprisingly good.

"It's only good today because of our supply run," Seamus said as if hearing the question.

Once the stew was thoroughly consumed, Lucy wiped the dribbles from her mouth and then looked up at the tall, bulky frame of Seamus, noticing the gray tufts of hair sticking out from under his red headscarf. His kindly sea-green eyes looked on her sympathetically. A graying beard hiding a sun worn face gave him an air of wisdom.

"Please tell me about Anne," Lucy requested.

Silas wandered over to the duo. "From your surprise, I gather you didn't know she was a pirate."

"No, when she looked surprised at the word 'pirate' she thought we said Anne was a 'pretty rat,'" Seamus said sarcastically.

"I'm just starting the conversation off."

"Please, stay focused. I need to know about Anne Bonny," Lucy broke in before the bickering got too far. "I've gone my whole life knowing nothing about my heritage, and then you two tell me you knew my mother and that she was a pirate."

Silas had been regarding his hands folded in his lap, inspecting every line, until Lucy paused. He raised his sober gray eyes to her face. "You are right; you deserve to know your own history." Silas turned and glanced at Seamus, who continued.

"Anne was a fiery and brave woman, the greatest leader we ever had. She could swear with the foulest mouth, drink a man twice her size under the table, and wreak fear into any crew in the Caribbean." Seamus smiled with his reveries of the past.

Silas took over from this point. "Back in those days we stormed many a Spanish ship. They were heavily loaded with gold or silver from the Spanish Main. Anne was always at the head of the charge, her axe waving in one hand and a pistol aimed in the other. She only wore men's clothing when we attacked. She said they were more freeing to wage battle in. Her pantaloons would billow in the sea wind, and her red curls would whip around her face like the head of Medusa. Aye, she was a sight to behold. "

Seamus's face fell as the memories became too hard to confront any longer. Silent tears streaked down his cheeks. Silas returned from the past and placed his hand on his friend's shoulder in solidarity. "Lucy, the past is still too raw to revisit. Events occurred that we are neither proud of nor can change, and we wish to forget, so we can't give you more than that for the moment. I'm sorry lassie. We do want to tell you about the past, and I thought we were ready to talk, but it's just too hard." He turned away from Lucy to his distraught comrade.

"Silas, why are we here to suffer? All that humans accomplish in their haphazard lives is death," Seamus questioned in his despair.

"Death, the only human accomplishment? How could you speak so ignorantly? Have you missed the advent of the printing press, the works of Aristotle, and the artistry of the Sistine Chapel? Human thought, creation, and innovation is why we are here." Silas's voice rose in his attempt to distract and raise the spirits of his friend.

Not wishing to disturb the two men any longer, Lucy quietly stood up and moved to the bow of the ship. The sun blazed its final glory of the day as it slipped beneath the ocean, leaving behind a trail of golden glitter on the clear blue sea that stretched out to the edge of the horizon. Lucy stood gazing out at this scene with her hands resting on the ship's railing, letting her mind wander to years before her birth, with images of a wild woman in men's breeches exchanging blows with sailors in fear of their lives crowding her mind. She'd almost forgotten where she was until she was jolted from the past by Sebastian's smooth voice.

"Couldn't take anymore of the arguing, huh?" By this time Silas and Seamus were engrossed in a passionate argument about the nature of human existence, the ghosts of the past no longer haunting them.

"Are they always like that?" Lucy asked glancing at the odd duo. "They don't seem like pirates."

"They've been like that as long as we've served together—constantly engaged in philosophical discourse. Before they joined this crew they served under Calico Jack Rackham, which is the crew that Anne Bonny served on. There was another woman too, Mary Read. Rackham's crew was legendary for the two women who dressed like men and fought as hard as any rogues of the sea."

"What happened to the crew?"

"Rackham was hung, Mary died in prison, and no one knows for sure what happened to Anne. Silas and Seamus never talk about it. And as you can see, they love to talk, so something awful and painful must have happened," Sebastian informed her compassionately.

"How did they...I mean they seem like well-educated men...how are they pirates?" Lucy asked curiously.

Sebastian grazed his right hand over the dark stubble on his cheek as he contemplated this question. "All men join this life for their own reasons, mostly for the freedom it gives. You'd be surprised where some of them came from: runaway slaves, displaced Indians, disgruntled subjects of the Crown, mistreated sailors. We've got men from all walks of life aboard. Silas and Seamus were doctors in their former lives, trained at Cambridge, both of them. Apparently, they met at Cambridge and have been arguing ever since. Anyway, they were on a ship sailing towards Boston from Edinburgh when they were overtaken and forced into service on Blackbeard's vessel in 1700. Doctors are always in short supply and badly needed on a pirate ship. Infection and disease set in easily and then destroy the crew. At that time Silas and Seamus were angry about the usurpation of King James from the thrown of England, as many true Scots were, so they were already on the outs with the government and took to the pirate life.

Once their time on Blackbeard's ship was complete, they joined up with Rackham. And then with the previous captain of this ship."

"You talk of freedom, but these men were forced into service. How is that a life of freedom?" Lucy asked skeptically.

"The sea gives you the freedom that society doesn't. We make our own rules here and don't have to follow someone else's. We have our own code that affirms the equality of each member of the crew. Not even I am above the law on this ship. The men have the right to oust me and maroon me on a deserted island if I go against the best interest of the crew."

Lucy pondered this response for a moment before hesitantly asking her next question. Sebastian's blue eyes were looking at her intently, as if waiting for her question. "How did you find yourself the captain of a crew of pirates?"

Rather than answering, Sebastian began unbuttoning his shirt.

"Sir, I do not think my question deserves such an impertinent response."

Sebastian grinned. "I suppose there weren't too many men in the convent?" Sebastian had dispensed with the last button and turned his back to Lucy, pulling the shirt down, revealing numerous, puffy, red welts from the base of his neck to the waistline of his pants. Lucy stepped back in revulsion at the sight.

"Cat-o-nine, crafted so the scars never heal. Ghastly isn't it?"

"Is this why you are a pirate?"

Sebastian was in the process of refastening his buttons as he explained. "I was commissioned to the *HMS Queen's Revenge* by my father at the age of seventeen. Life on a naval vessel is all about rules and regulations, and the captain's word is law. We were en route to the Carolinas when a storm hit and threw us off course. We were lost for weeks and rations and water ran very low. The cabin boy, a lad of ten, became very weak and sick. I had become friends with him, teaching him to read on my nights off. He was all alone, and I couldn't stand to see him wasting away, becoming paler and more emaciated with every day, so I raided the remaining food stores and gave the boy an extra share of dried pork.

"The captain discovered this act of kindness, and I was shackled below deck for a day and then brought out on deck the following morning in front of the entire crew. The captain ordered the quartermaster to whip me twenty times with the cat-o-nine. The first lash of the nine knotted ropes snapped and bit into my skin. I could hear it ripping open, and the pain was blinding. After about the tenth lash, I passed out. I woke up a day later with a throbbing, bloody back. I couldn't lie on my back for weeks.

"Shortly after this episode, Captain Wallace and his pirate vessel the *Peril* came upon us and so terrified the naval crew with canon fire, wild cries, and waving cutlasses that the captain of the *HMS Queen's Revenge* surrendered before a single death occurred. Captain Wallace came aboard and asked if any of the navy men wanted to join his pirate crew. I didn't even hesitate, never looked back, and never regretted my decision to leave the navy. Twelve other crew members defected with me."

Lucy inspected this man before her, a suddenly far more interesting object. A compassionate renegade? Her chocolate eyes met his with understanding. "How then did you become captain? You are yet so young."

"Young in years, old in battle," Sebastian softly replied. "The crew voted me captain after Captain Wallace died of an infection from a bullet wound to his stomach. He treated me as a son, and I worked hard for the crew and the ship, earning the respect of the men." Sebastian whipped off his tricorn hat and made a graceful bow towards Lucy. "And that, Miss Cormac, is how I became the master of this motley band of ruffians."

Lucy smiled at this faux gallantry. The high-pitched cry of a fiddle filtered through the night air, starting as a melodic lullaby and moving into a frantic reel as clapping and shouting accompanied the musician. Several raw voices took up the tune in a raucous song.

Sebastian presented his hand to Lucy and asked, "*Mademoiselle*, would you care to dance; even though we are a band of vicious renegades, we are excellent dancers. And it is not often that we have an actual woman aboard to dance with. Although, Seamus doesn't look half bad in a dress, if you can believe it," Sebastian joked.

Lucy laughed but hesitated at his offered hand. She had never danced, especially not with a gentleman, but the music was catchy, the stars brilliant in the clear night sky, and the gentleman in front of her, not as bad as she once thought. She placed her hand in his. "I've never danced before; it wasn't a typical evening's entertainment amongst the nuns, but neither was associating with pirates…"

The pair joined the crowd around Silas and his fiddle. Sebastian placed a firm calloused hand on the small of Lucy's back and took her right hand in his warm left palm. Bridging the gap between them, Sebastian pulled his partner towards him, just inches from his chest, in a strong grasp. Lucy awkwardly moved with Sebastian's swaying body, keeping her eyes on her feet. The pace quickened to a reel; there was no more time to look at her feet. She allowed herself to be whisked along with the intoxicating cries of the fiddle. With a beaming smile, Lucy picked up the folds of her dress to keep from tripping and held on for the rollicking ride in the strong arms of her partner.

Chapter 9

Lucy lay in bed beside Gracie, soundly sleeping next to her, playing over the exhilaration of dancing on deck with Sebastian in her head. The fact that Sebastian had kindly given up his quarters to the only two women the *Peril* had ever housed for a hammock in the hold of the ship with the other sailors and that she was now in the very bed that Sebastian slept in each night, only brought his image more clearly to her mind. She blushed at this indelicate thought and blushed even more deeply when she thought of her hand in his and the warmth radiating from his hand into her back. But she'd sobered from this fantasy with the remembrance that he was in fact a pirate who'd probably killed countless innocents in his days on the sea, which then brought her back to the realization that her mother too was a pirate who had taken many lives and plundered numerous ships at sea. Less than twenty years ago it could have been her mother that boarded the ship she stowed away on, seizing sugar and rum and threatening the crew with an axe and a cutlass.

These thoughts flashed back and forth through her head, plaguing her late into the night. Just as her brain finally found peace and her eyes closed in exhaustion, the ship began to list, at first gently and then with more urgency. The rocking roused both Lucy and Gracie. The rocking of the ship became so extreme that the two women were nearly hurled from the bed. It seemed as if the ship would just dive right to the bottom of the sea. The only chair in the chamber, and the only piece of furniture that didn't seem to be nailed down, screeched across the floor until it finally tumbled over from its efforts. The clatter of the chair in the dark would have been more pronounced except that rain began to violently pelt the outside of the *Peril*, and the wind rose with a frenzied intent to rip the ship in twain. The sound of God's fury engulfing the bobbing boat had the full attention of the two women, who were both clinging to each other and the bed to steady themselves in the tumult.

"*Mon Dieu,* I think I'm going to be sick," moaned Gracie. "I haven't spent much time on a ship before, but this can't be good."

"No, not at all Gracie," and with that, Lucy threw up over the side of the bed. She wiped her mouth. "I can't stay trapped in here. I need some air."

"We could die out there Lucy. We are safer in here," reasoned Gracie.

"I think I'll die in here just as easily," Lucy eked out as she vomited again in rhythm to the aggressive tossing of the ship.

"Ok then, at least we'll see death coming from out there in the open. Dying entombed in the cabin of a ship wasn't what I envisioned freedom looking like," Gracie resolved.

The women abandoned Sebastian's quarters and made their way to the deck as carefully as they could, but with the shroud of darkness and the lurching of the ship, the simple task of walking became taxing. On the other side of the shelter of the captain's cabin chaos reigned, with sailors running from post to post, tearing down sails and attempting to secure the ship amongst a deluge of rain, flashes of lightening, and wind whipping like angry tentacles at man, ship, and sea alike. The waves lashed at the seemingly minuscule ship now being thrown from one white cap to another. A cloak of blackness covered the sea, engulfing the scurrying people on board the powerless vessel. Orders rang out every so often over the cry of the wind and anger of the sea.

"Secure the main sail!"

"Keep her head to the sea!"

"Take in the small sails!"

One sailor had climbed to the heights of the main mast and was preparing to pull the topsail in, when a loud clap of thunder rang out, promptly followed by a blinding flash of lightening just off the bow of the ship. The action threw the sailor off his bearings, and Lucy and Gracie watched in horror as he plummeted into the boiling sea, sinking into the abyss. "Help him, help him! Quickly he's fallen into the sea! Please, help him!" Lucy screamed at the top of her lungs to anyone who might listen.

From the quarter deck came a booming command, "Miss Cormac take the wheel, now! I'll find Sturges!" Lucy and Gracie navigated the steps leading to the helm now running with water, clasping hands for strength and balance. As soon as Lucy's hand touched the wheel, Sebastian rushed off, only yelling over his shoulder as he ran in the direction of the fallen sailor, "Keep her steady. By the way, what the hell are you two doing out here?"

Lucy attempted to keep the ship on course through the turbulent waves, but the unrelenting motion of the waves rendered her useless. "I can't hold on. Gracie, help me," Lucy commanded as she bent over and emptied her stomach on the deck.

"Lucy, breathe. Just take a moment and breathe. We will survive. I'll be damned if I die here tonight, and since I need your help, you can't die either. So hold on!" Lucy looked up at the rain-drenched, black hair plastered to Gracie's determined face and willed herself to stand erect in the face of the storm.

"You're right; we've both come too far to die now. We even survived a pirate attack. We'll survive this storm too."

As the women strained against the sea, they could just barely decipher Silas by the port side of the vessel attempting to tie down the fore boom. His fingers slipped with the constant wet, and his feet were unsteady beneath him, both making his errand more difficult. So engrossed in his mission was he that Silas neglected to notice a sudden shift in the ship, which swung the mighty boom, smacking him square in the back and knocking him off his feet completely, sending him over the side. But before his expected plunge into the depths, Silas reached out his hands, and in a moment of luck, grabbed the rope that he'd been toiling with earlier. He screamed for help as the dark waves lapped at his legs, doggedly trying to pull him into the sea.

Gracie heard the scream over the wail of the wind. Lucy noticed nothing as she was retching once again, while hanging diligently to the wheel. Through a flash of lightening Gracie spied the older man's head bobbing off the side of the ship where he had been standing just moments earlier. "Hold tight Lucy. I'll be right back." Gracie left her comrade and sprinted towards the man dangling off the deck.

"Calme-toi! J'suis là," Gracie yelled as she threw herself down on the deck, grabbing onto the railing to steady herself, and then reached for the rope with the dangling sailor. *"Bouge pas!"* Silas stared up into the sopping wet face of his rescuer and thought for the second time in his life how lucky it was to have a woman aboard ship. Gracie wrapped her strong fingers around the thick rope and then pulled with all her weight. Inch by inch, Gracie

widened the gap between Silas and the angry sea, until he slithered safely back on deck. Both Gracie and Silas flopped on the deck in exhaustion. From the wheel, Gracie could hear Lucy yelling, "Well done Gracie, well done," in between vomiting.

As Silas gulped in what he thought briefly might have been his last breaths, he managed to exclaim, "*Ma cherie* Gracie, you're not a bad sort to have aboard ship. For saving my rather useless life, I am forever in your debt my girl." Silas patted the girl sprawled on the deck next to him fondly on the arm. He was thankful that his years of education in Europe, and later his years as a scourge in the French Caribbean, made it possible to thank the girl for his life in her native tongue of French. Gracie smiled at Silas as her breathing returned to normal. Silas, seeing that the storm had not yet abated and that he must return to his seaman duties, rose to his feet with noticeable effort; he wasn't as spry as in his former days and his back was killing him. He grunted in defiance of that reality. He extended his hand to Gracie and pulled her to her feet. "My dear, we must return to battle. No rest for the weary, as they say." Silas patted her one last time on the back and pushed back into the sheets of rain to return to that blasted boom.

Gracie returned to Lucy at the helm. Lucy beamed at the returning hero. "And they say that women are bad luck on a pirate ship."

"Maybe we're the ones that caused the storm," Gracie said dryly.

"Believe what you will Gracie, but the truth is that you saved a life today, so I say that's good luck my friend."

The two women continued to hold the wheel as steady as they could through the next hours, until the storm could rage no more and spluttered to a halt. Lucy and Gracie both sighed with relief as they saw the first glimmer of sunlight peaking through the thick clouds, breaking the seemingly endless dark. The rain ceased, the winds lessened, the seas calmed, and the *Peril* relaxed into the easy rhythm of the water. Suddenly, it was as if the storm had never been, only the drenched shipmates, soaked deck, and debris strewn willy-nilly over the deck gave evidence to the wild night they had all passed.

With the end of the storm, Sebastian returned to the helm of the ship. "You did well," he praised his new crew, "but I repeat, what the hell are you doing up here in a storm?"

Lucy responded with a bit of venom, "I wasn't going to stay in your quarters and die in my own vomit, thank you very much. Besides, it seems you needed the help out here. What happened to the man who fell overboard?"

Sebastian lowered his head in respect. "Sturges. I never found him. The sea took him. He was a fine sailor. Been on this ship long before me."

"I'm sorry Captain."

"It's the risk of the sea and really the only place any true sailor would want to die. Here, let me take the helm back. You look a little green. Maybe you should sit a spell. Both of you look tired." Sebastian reached for the wheel and, in so doing, brushed Lucy's hand as she released the helm to its rightful owner.

At his sudden touch, Lucy stammered, "I may not be cut out for this life of the sea. Every bit of that delicious stew is now littered on the deck."

"I was green for weeks the first time I went to sea. I couldn't keep a morsel of food down and lost a lot of weight before I got my sea legs. Yours will come in time," Sebastian encouraged.

"Captain Strongbow, did you hear how Gracie saved Silas? You might have lost two men tonight if it hadn't been for her," Lucy trumpeted her friend's heroics.

Sebastian appraised Gracie and remarked, "I had not heard of this great feat."

Lucy began to excitedly recount the great rescue, adding in a few embellishments where they seemed appropriate. At the end of the retelling Sebastian smiled approvingly at Gracie.

"Gracie, I thank you for your bravery and the life of Silas. He's been a great friend and mentor to me over the years. If there

is anything I can do for you, let me know; I am your servant."
Sebastian bowed like a gentleman, proof of his words.

Gracie turned her head away shyly, not used to so much praise and attention; insults and disregard she was used to, not this. "It was only what I should have done, what anyone should have done," she modestly said to no one in particular.

"Be that as it may, you were the one who did it, and for your efforts I offer you protection, as well as you, Miss Cormac, for keeping us on course through the storm despite your stomach. You both make fine pirates," Sebastian grinned. And even with, or maybe because of, the thick blondish curls still drenched with rain and the white linen shirt glued with wet to his well-built torso; that grin poured into Lucy and erased every concern of the past few hours, and like the sun's effect on the rain, dried up her last remnant of fear.

Chapter 10

It was a relief to see a slew of vivid yellow, pink, and white houses appear on the horizon as the *Peril* approached the town of Nassau on the island of New Providence, the most popular of the Bahamian island cluster for those in the pirate occupation. The motley crew was noticeably excited at the prospects that were to greet them on shore after months of deprivation; they had even weathered a severe storm. They had earned their dues. Drink in plenty, women to excess, and a soft place to sleep all could be bought with the sales from the spoils of multiple scores. Sailors fondly looked forward to a rendezvous with Rosemarie, Veronique, or Suzanne.

Lucy too could feel anticipation coursing through her veins. Here she would meet this Lafitte. Maybe he could finally tell her where her mother had hidden away for all these long years. As the sapphire blue Caribbean waters receded and the pastel colored buildings and docks grew larger, Lucy couldn't help but think of Anne arriving at this very same place twenty years ago with a lout for a husband and piracy in her future. *What possibly had driven her to that life?* Lucy wondered.

Sebastian waited at a distance, not watching the city grow closer, but watching this woman stare off in daydreams. In fact, for him, the approach of land meant Lucy would be leaving, a thought that actually sent a pain through his chest. But he pushed this spasm to the depths of his gut, knowing that she would never wish to stay aboard a pirate ship with an outlaw. He couldn't stay away from her before she left though, so he strode towards Lucy.

"Do you think this Lafitte will lead you to your mother?"

Anne was startled by Sebastian's sudden presence. "I do not know. I hope that will be the case." Lucy's eyes wandered over the features of the tall captain whom she had grown rather fond of during this journey. "I thank you for bringing us safely to port, sir."

Sebastian blushed to think of the very real danger that Lucy had been in while on board his ship. "It was a pleasure."

She paused a moment considering her next favor, but decided that she did trust this pirate, and he might prove valuable to her search. "Captain Strongbow, I have another favor to ask of you. Will you accompany me to this Lafitte? I don't know what sort he is, but it might be a benefit to have an escort who can wield a sword, and as I recall, you did offer both Gracie and me protection for our valuable services to your ship."

69

Sebastian was taken aback by this request. But it was true that Nassau was not known as a civilized town, especially for women. And he was aware that the idea that Lucy needed his help and wanted to continue their acquaintance brought a sense of relief to him. There was nothing that could keep him from accompanying this woman on her mission, not even a promise that he had made years ago to never set foot on the island again. "I'll only accompany you if you stop calling me Captain Strongbow and call me by my Christian name, Sebastian."

"Aye, aye Captain Sebastian. You in turn must call me Lucy."

"Then, your wish is my command, my Lady Lucy." Sebastian bowed with a dramatic flourish. Lucy laughed at the absurd gesture and then stuck out her hand to the gentleman. Sebastian took the delicate hand offered to him and kissed it gently.

***

Her mind trained on her own search, Gracie followed Lucy, Sebastian and the Scots from the quay into the heart of Nassau at a gradually lengthening distance. As no one was paying any attention to her, she disappeared into the activity of town life.

However, Gracie was wrong that no one observed her disappearance. One man, who had been unloading boxes of tea off a cargo ship just in from London, was instantly distracted by the appearance of the daughter of Anne Bonny and a familiar slave girl. He followed them at a safe distance, and when the dark one broke off from the group, he stayed on her tail, a plan forming in his devilish mind.

***

The façade of the Rooster's Crow was worn and bespoke of years of abuse. The wooden sign with the emblem of a crowing rooster hanging over the door frame creaked back and forth in the slight breeze, and laughter oozed from the open door and windows. Lucy and Sebastian trailed behind Silas and Seamus. The Scots guided the group while loudly expostulating on the virtues of democratic versus monarchical forms of government. From within the pub a gleeful cry of, "Silas and Seamus, quit your incessant noise; we all know no government is the best government," emanated.

Laughter followed this faceless attack. At the door a tall, dark haired man with a black goatee appeared. Age was beginning to appear in the man as his once jet black hair was now speckled with white and lines had formed around his sparkling blue eyes. "My old friends, it's good to hear your over-opinionated voices again."

The friendly proprietor greeted Silas and Seamus with a shake of the hand and a clap on the back. "I see you have brought friends with you." He smiled warmly at the odd band, greeting

71

them with welcome and the promise of a free pint. "I am Lafitte, the owner of this fine establishment, and even though you keep these old kooks in your company, you are friends of mine." Lafitte took a second glance at Lucy, sensing familiarity in her presence, but not quite placing her, he ushered his guests inside the watering hole.

The inside of the Rooster's Crow hadn't changed much since the era of Anne Bonny. It was still a simple establishment with just a few tables and chairs, framed by plain wooden walls. There were no pictures or decorations on the walls. The color of the place was brought by the clientele. Most of the tables and the bar were filled with men of various demeanor; some with long beards, some missing an eye or a limb, some with knives strapped to their waistbands, some with pistols peering out of pockets, and all with hardened, weathered faces. A few women with frilly, garish outfits roamed around, serving drinks and entertaining the guests. There was much laughter, drinking, and storytelling happening at all the tables. Pirates away from the sea only had so much time to enjoy their leisure, so enjoy it to the fullest they did.

Lucy looked around at this dubious clientele and was very relieved that she was flanked by several men who were just as hardened as the worst of the carousing lot. Lafitte guided the group to a table, pulled five drafts of an amber brew from the tap behind the bar into large glasses and placed them before the travelers.

Sebastian introduced himself to the inn keeper and thanked Lafitte for his hospitality. He then receded into a chair to enjoy the pint and allow the conversation to turn to the subject at hand, that of Lucy's mysterious parentage.

Seamus took the brief pause to broach said subject. "Lafitte, you may notice this young woman with the determined stare to your right?"

"Yes, I have. You look familiar somehow, but I can't place it." Lafitte looked more carefully at the sculpt of the mouth, the curve of the neck, and the shape of the eyes of this woman impatiently fiddling with the buttons on her simple blue frock.

"Monsieur Lafitte, I am Lucy Cormac, and I believe I am the daughter of Anne Bonny. And from your expression I feel you recognize that name."

Lafitte's hand went to his goatee and stroked the hairs, while a smile spread across his face and the glistening of tears touched his eyes. "Can it be so?" he softly spoke. He leaped forward from his chair and embraced Lucy with his strong arms. "I always hoped I'd meet you again. You were such a tiny thing when last I saw you."

Lucy was overcome by the unexpected outpouring of emotion from this stranger. Lafitte pulled away from Lucy just

73

enough to inspect her face. "You've grown into a lovely young woman. Where did you come from?"

"I grew up in a convent in Martinique."

"The daughter of a notorious pirate amongst the nuns of a convent. *Incroyable.*" Lafitte laughed heartily at this news.

"The nuns treated me very well and gave me a good home for seventeen years," Lucy responded indignantly.

"I'm sure they did. And I'm glad of it. What brings you to the Rooster's Crow? It's not exactly up to the standards of a nun."

"Silas and Seamus said you might know where this Anne Bonny might be found."

Lafitte looked away from the eyes that were intently looking at him, pleading for information. He knew but was sworn to secrecy.

"No my child I do not know where Anne is," he lied convincingly, as he had practiced so often. "I haven't seen her in seventeen years." This was true. Lafitte hadn't seen his good friend since the birth of Lucy. He had missed her every day since.

Lucy's heart sank, a lump formed in her throat, and hope evaporated. She could barely speak. "Monsieur Lafitte, if you can't tell me where she is, can you tell me about Anne's life here on New Providence? I know she lived here at the Rooster's Crow with a man named James Bonny after they left the Carolinas. I even met this Bonny on Martinique."

74

Silas and Seamus simultaneously spit out mouthfuls of beer. "You never mentioned anything about Bonny to us before," Silas choked out.

"Horrible creature he is," Seamus shuttered in memory.

"Yes, I've had the pleasure. What I don't understand is why he hates Anne Bonny so much."

"Still spiteful after all these years. That sounds like Bonny alright, holding a grudge to the end," Lafitte exchanged a knowing look with Silas and Seamus. "As most good grudges, this one has to do with love and betrayal."

Being the storyteller he was, with a rapt audience, Lafitte began his story of love and betrayal.

Chapter 11

New Providence 1717

Anne had grown weary of her husband; he paid her no attention, but only used her money for his own drink and often disappeared for many days at a time with a band of slave traffickers, that is, when he wasn't playing informant. The men she met in the Rooster's Crow were far more attentive and interesting to her. She spent more and more time carousing with her new friends, partaking in pints when sailors came in to port after weeks away.

On one of these very nights, Anne was sloshing back a dram or two of whiskey over the tales of the high seas with Lafitte and his amore, a muscular, square jawed pirate with rich, deep black skin named Simon Callow.

She had grown to love Lafitte and considered him a confidante. They had both taken to trading secrets during those hours of clean-up after the rowdy customers had been finally kicked out. Anne described her childhood, the unfortunate death of the maid Henny and her naïve mistake to run away with Bonny. Lafitte in turn shared the more colorful events of his life.

One such colorful event was Simon Callow. Simon was one of the unfortunates who had been shipped to the Bahamas as human cargo and sold for hard labor. He lingered in that state for two years before escaping by swimming to one of the numerous deserted cays that lay not far off the main islands of the Bahamas. It was while grilling a fish over a camp fire on that cay that the *Revenge* dropped anchor. Many of the crew had formerly been slaves too, so Simon fit right in with the band of pirates and joined them.

Lafitte waxed on and on about Simon. How he was so smitten with this man because of the great depth of his soul. "I lift him up with my innate cheerfulness; he anchors me to the earth with his melancholy," Lafitte had repeated more than once or twice, to which Anne would laugh at Lafitte's sappy poeticism.

At the present moment, Lafitte was gleefully relating a gory tale to Simon and Anne of the sinking of a Spanish galleon off the coast of Jamaica and the riches that lay beneath the sea in sunken treasure, when in entered a well-dressed gentleman. The buckle on his black boots gleamed; the white, silk stockings showed off his muscular calves; the black knee-breeches were highlighted with a leather scabbard sheathing an ornately handled sword at his side; a smart tricorn hat perched on his head; a well-trimmed black beard half covered his face. But the most remarkable piece of the ensemble was the unusual calico waistcoat that attracted every gaze and accentuated the gentleman's strut. Following close behind this veritable peacock were four brutes that paled in the light of their leader.

Over the top of the pint glass poised at her lips, Anne's gaze caught on this stranger. With his appearance, she lost all interest in Lafitte's story. Anne looked the dandy up and down, from his shiny black boots, to his golden belt buckle, to his honey eyes. She slowly placed the glass on the table and turned to Lafitte. Anne tapped him on the shoulder in mid-sentence.

"Lafitte, who is this man at the door with the calico waistcoat?"

Both Lafitte and Simon turned their attention to the gentleman and his entourage making their way to a table in the corner of the pub. Lafitte smiled, "Does he strike your fancy *Cherie Rouge*?"

"That is my captain. Captain Rackham," Simon announced gruffly in an English flavored with an African accent.

Lafitte jumped in with more detail when it was obvious that Simon wasn't going to elaborate further. "A true rascal of the sea and a captain to boot. Captain Calico Jack Rackham. They call him Calico Jack because…"

"He's so fond of a calico waistcoat?" Anne cut in wryly. Lafitte rolled his eyes in assent.

"A captain and a fine swagger," Anne mused.

"Yes a fine 'swagger,' I saw where your eyes paused," Lafitte teased.

Anne gulped down another swig of beer and then strode to Captain Rackham's table.

"Captain, would you and your men care for a pint?"

Rackham, interrupted in his discussion with his crew, faced the confident voice. *Who was this serving wench who dared to interrupt his meeting with his men?* Rackham was used to giving orders and people, both men and women, waiting on his every word. This wench had a haughty air, but a fine figure and daring eyes that taunted him. She did not cower when his fierce disdain attempted to cow her. *This wench might be worth a romp after several pints.*

"Girl, do you not see we are in private conversation?"

"Yes, but you look as though you have a thirst."

"Since you have the nerve to interrupt our business, we'll take four of your finest ales." He dug into his pocket and pulled out a handful of gold coins. "That should adequately compensate."

"Those are Spanish if I'm bloody well not mistaken. Have you been hunting Spanish galleons?"

"You ask questions that shouldn't be asked girl. My business is none of yours, and I suggest you keep it that way."

Anne was not broken by these harsh commands; she was not easily deterred from her prize once set upon, and this flamboyant captain had become her prize. He would bend to her, as long as she didn't give in to his commanding ways.

"Did you find your coins off the coast of Jamaica? I hear there are still treasures to be found from the storms ten years ago that sank a Spanish Armada from Peru." *I must remember to thank Lafitte for sharing that useful tale*, she thought.

Rackham was at a loss for words. He was struck dumb first by this wench's refusal to back down and, secondly, for her knowledge.

"You have heard stories in this place I see. You weary me with your chatter. Fetch us our pints woman."

"I do not fetch," and with that, Anne abruptly turned and walked back to her table and rejoined her drinking partners. She left Rackham and his men thirsty and dumbfounded. Rackham was particularly surprised at this behavior. No woman had ever dared say no. They feared his wrath, but this mere barkeep had said no and walked away. He was intrigued at this unexpected show of bravery. The swarthy gentleman pounded his palm on the table, shaking it violently as he rose from his bench. With purpose, he strode towards Anne.

"Woman," he bellowed, silencing the carousing, "you are insolent and should not be a server, so I invite you to partake in a pint with me. We can further talk on Spanish gold."

Anne toyed with the mug that sat in front of her and pondered this request. She gave a quick, conspiratorial dart of her eye to Lafitte and then replied curtly, "I'd prefer a whiskey."

From that day on, Rackham and Anne were inseparable. At the Rooster's Crow they were seen huddled in a booth plotting attacks on the Spanish fleets that sailed up and down the coast. News of his cuckolding got round to Bonny quickly, which culminated in a brawl outside the Rooster's Crow between Bonny and his comrades and Rackham's battle ready crew. The skirmish was over not long after it had begun. James Bonny narrowly survived the encounter with a broken arm and several broken ribs. Rackham received a black eye and Anne a bump on the head. Bonny receded into the shadows, relinquishing his hold on his wife, and Anne became permanently affixed to Calico Jack. A tentative peace followed, at least for now.

Bonny had other concerns at the moment anyway. Discovering the money to be made in ratting out former comrades, he had turned informant on his pirate friends. Seeing as he was privy to much information through his connections at the Rooster's Crow, this business was quite lucrative for him. If a certain gentleman didn't buy Bonny a pint or looked at him the wrong way, he ended up in prison or with a stretched neck.

Times were changing in New Providence as the governorship had changed to Woodes Rogers, a young admiral of

81

the British navy whose sole goal in the islands was to clean up the trash and tame the wild habits of the renegades that called the Bahamas home. With a more civilized and law abiding citizenry, wealthy landowners would move in, suiting the needs of the crown. Governor Rogers came in with an iron fist and thousands of pounds worth of bribes to coax the locals into informing. Bonny quickly took the Governor up on his need for information and lined his pockets with the betrayal of former friends.

***

Change was on the horizon in the colony, but for Anne and Rackham, that change was still years away. Anne took to the seas with Captain Rackham on board his battle scarred skiff the *Revenge*. She wore men's pants, a baggy shirt that concealed her bosom, and a red waistcoat. At her sides, strapped to her belt, resided a small hatchet to the right and a pistol to the left. Anne had unintentionally trained for battle throughout her life. She learned to shoot muskets and pistols on her father's farm by stealing her father's weapons and running off into the woods for target practice. She often came back with rabbits to add to the kitchen surplus. The fact that it was all done without her father's knowledge made it all the more exciting. During her stay at the Rooster's Crow, she had learned the finer art of sword play from Lafitte, who was an expert in the sport. The two spent hours after closing the pub clashing swords. And most importantly, she had fight; boy did she have fight and fury. For the first time in Anne's life she would have the freedom to use the skills that came so naturally to her.

Even though Anne dressed as a man, she didn't hide the fact that she was indeed a woman. At times she hid her trademark red locks under a blue head scarf, but often she let her thick hair blow wildly in the sea wind. Generally, she put her hair away as a practicality of ship board work or battle. The enemy feared a pistol wielding man more than a girl holding a gun.

The entire crew, however, knew that Anne was the Captain's woman. Anne liked to flaunt her femininity in front of the crew by wearing lacy, red dresses. The crew in general feared the presence of a woman on board the ship; superstitions ran deep at sea, and a woman always brought bad luck, and bad luck at sea always spelled disaster. So the crew ignored this woman who dared dress as a man. There were grumblings amongst the crew; rumors began to spread that Anne was a witch, had bewitched their captain and would curse them all to the deeps. Simon was on friendly terms with Anne, but considering he rarely said more than a gruff word or two to anyone, he wasn't much help in winning over the crew. But it was no matter to Anne. She laughed at the superstitions and rumors; she was having the time of her life, and she was the captain's woman. The other sailors couldn't do anything more than give her dirty looks.

One morning, after two weeks at sea, the *Revenge* was rounding a rock outcropping along the coast of Bermuda, when the sailor on watch, a young boy of eighteen, with the fresh blond facial hair of youth, yelled out, "Sloop off the starboard bow...300 knots."

At the sound of the alarm, Rackham joined the crew to spy on the unsuspecting ship. At his side, Silas pulled out his spy glass, and looking into it, announced, "She's French by the look of the flag. Looks like a private merchant ship."

"Are you sure Silas? The shape of the bow looks like a war ship," Seamus suggested.

"I am sure. Do you have the glass? No. There are no guns on the sides," Silas refuted.

"Men, to your stations. Ready all weapons and prepare to board." The command reached over the frenzied chatter in the air and instantly sent the crew scattering over the deck of the ship, some to the hull to gather pistols and some to man the canons. Anne, with her pistol held tightly in her left hand and the hatchet at the ready in her swinging hand, stood beside Rackham, as they watched the vessel grow closer.

"If she's indeed French, she'll be coming from the southern islands. Most likely laden with sugar and rum. Not gold, but still worth a great deal," Rackham informed her. Anne felt slightly disappointed that gold wouldn't be their quarry, but her hand gripped the hatchet, flexing over the handle in anticipation of the fight that lay ahead.

Rackham noticed this movement. "I see you're excited, anxious for a fight my wild woman. Remain calm or you'll be run through."

The prey reached within distance of the cannons of the *Revenge*. Rackham sent out the command, "Simon, show them our colors." In an instant, a black flag with Rackham's trademark skull flanked by two crossed sabers was flapping boldly in the wind high above the vessel—the Jolly Roger, scourge of the seas. "Now run out the guns Mr. Short. Fire one over their stern."

Almost immediately, the violent rip of the cannon ball exploded from the starboard of the ship. The iron ball hurtled through the air, sailed over the stern of the French ship, and landed with a splash on the other side. Sailors scurried around the deck, shouting orders as they ran.

On the deck of the *Revenge*, the fiercely armed crew had also gathered and sent out a vicious war cry. Blades and pistols flashed in the sun as the warriors waved their weapons and screamed with a murderous rage at what they believed were their unprepared prey. But to the astonishment of the pirates, soldiers clad in blue, with bayonets at the ready, marched out to the deck of the French ship and posted themselves in preparation for an assault. Simultaneously, the gunner doors opened, exposing the dark iron mouths of the cannons.

"Silas, I told you it was a warship," Seamus grumbled.

"No you didn't, you only asked if it was. And at that time, the gunner holes were closed. And, it's not a warship. It's just under military protection," Silas countered defensively.

"Protection from us, but it's no matter. There are only ten soldiers on board compared to our forty," Rackham urged. "Sugar and rum men. Tonight we'll be drunk off our booty." A cry rang out. "Bring the bow round and ready yourselves to board," he commanded.

The first shots came from the French, which were followed by a return volley by the crew of the *Revenge*. Screams of pain rang out on both sides as bullets hit arms, legs, and chests. Several pirates fell, gasping for air. Blood spurted and pooled on the deck.

Anne stood at the front firing shot after shot at the French, yelling with the fury of hell behind her.

The ships came within several feet of each other, and the outlaws leaped the gamut, never pausing in their slashing. Anne leaped too, at the side of Rackham, with her hatchet held aloft. She lashed out at any limbs that came in her path, crippling several soldiers. Within thirty minutes the fight was over. Seven French were dead and five pirates. Anne, Silas, and Seamus held the

French captain and his officers at pistol point, as the humiliated captain surrendered the ship.

With the ship secured, the pirates ventured off to scavenge supplies from the cargo, while Anne tied and gagged the captain in his quarters. With the captain immobilized, Anne began inspecting his chamber for anything of value. She found a belt buckle made of gold, a stash of a few gold coins, a ruby ring inscribed with best wishes from a lover, and the captain's private stash of wine— something called "Champagne." Thinking there was nothing more of note, Anne stuffed her findings in a sack and was about to leave the poor wriggling captain to his fate, when a sizable chest hidden under the captain's bed caught her eye. Seeing that Anne was making her way to the chest, the captain began to thrash more violently, attempting to free himself from his bonds, but it was no use. Anne pulled the iron chest from its hiding place and inspected her find.

The chest was secured with a giant lock, and the frame itself was forged by impenetrable metal. Anne turned on the bound man, "The key monsieur; tell me where the key is," Anne demanded and took out the Frenchman's gag.

He glared at her, trying desperately to preserve his last ounce of dignity.

"That is not the correct response. Let's see…is the key around your neck?" Anne tore at the man's clothes until his neck was visible, but she found no key. She patted down his pockets, but felt nothing remotely like a key. Becoming irritated, Anne slapped the captain in the face and once again demanded, "Tell me where to find the key. You have no other option. This chest is now mine, and I'm not leaving without the key to the lock." The prisoner held his ground and spit on his tormentor in response.

Anne grew furious and screamed insult upon insult on the captive. *How dare this man ignore her commands*? Upon hearing the commotion, two men appeared at the door, the men called Silas and Seamus. They were two men that Anne could not as of yet tell apart—one was taller than the other, but they both talked a lot. "What have we here?" one of them inquired.

"None of your business louts. I've got this in hand," Anne snapped back. She pulled a blood-stained hatchet from her belt. She pressed it to her captive's stomach, and moving the deadly blade slowly upward, she popped off one brass button, and then another and another until the pernicious edge had only one more button to sever before reaching the soft flesh of his neck. "One last button and then you are dead, and I still take the chest."

"This does not look good for the captain, now does it Silas? One bottle of whiskey says she slays the poor fellow," Seamus quipped to his comrade while they both looked on in admiration at the scene unfolding in front of their eyes, care of the newest member of the crew.

"I say she doesn't have it in her. I'll raise the stakes to two bottles of whiskey," Silas countered.

Meanwhile, the poor gentleman, whose neck was in question, looked on the approaching hatchet with wide eyes filled with terror; his brow sweat profusely, and his knees shook audibly. At the last moment he found it beneficial to utter, "My boot."

Anne laughed in triumph and removed the deadly hatchet. She forced the man's polished black boots off his feet and dumped each to the floor. The precious key clattered to the floor. Barely able to contain her excitement, Anne took the key, inserted it in the lock, and turned. It clicked and opened. She pulled open the heavy lid and gasped at the glitter of countless French silver coins.

Silas and Seamus drew closer to view the wondrous treasure and both inhaled. "That is worth more than the sum of the rest of the cargo," Silas mused with eyes glazing over.

"Now you two bystanders can make yourselves useful and help me haul this out of here," Anne demanded.

Silas and Seamus looked on this formidable woman with new admiration and saluted. "Aye, aye. At your service," Seamus mocked.

As the pirates exited in glee over the bounty of silver, Anne couldn't help returning to the captain, who tensed with fear again at the ruthless pirate's approach, until, instead of a knife plunging into his gut, the Frenchman found his assailant's lips firmly planted on his in thank you. She laughed and ran off after her confederates, leaving the captain even further perplexed at being kissed by a pirate with very soft lips.

***

It didn't take long for Silas and Seamus to sing the praises of Anne and recount to the entire crew the sight of the poor captain losing his buttons, and nearly his head, and the recovery of the greatest prize of the day by the fiercest woman to ever sail the seas. Murmurings of Anne bringing bad luck to the ship quickly turned to Anne being the best luck that ever fell on the crew of the *Revenge.*

Chapter 12

New Providence 1738

Silas and Seamus sat with their drinks in hand, grins spread wide on their faces with the memories of that great day of pillaging, helmed by Rackham and Anne.

"That was a fruitful day," Seamus remembered. "We took six barrels of Labatt Rum and drank until the next day."

"Anne also took a fiddle from that poor, frightened captain and played until dawn," Silas chimed in. "The same fiddle I have now," he added.

"I remember. She could make that fiddle sing. When morale was low on the ship, after weeks at sea, Anne got that fiddle out, and, suddenly, the crew was miles away."

Lucy listened to these memories of the mother she never met. She had felt so many emotions through this story, but what stood out the most was the identity of Captain Calico Jack Rackham.

Lucy twisted the ring around her finger several times, pulled it off her finger and murmured the inscription, "*Always My*

Bonny-R," quietly aloud and tried to picture the two people that this bauble had bonded. "R" must stand for Rackham; the pieces were starting to fall into place. *Could he be my father*, she thought to herself, not ready to say it out loud.

Sebastian however couldn't keep himself from asking exactly what Lucy was thinking. It was possible that she was the daughter of pirate royalty, the two most well-known pirates of the Golden Age of Piracy. "Is Lucy's father Captain Rackham?"

Silas and Seamus looked at each other nervously. Lafitte mulled over his whiskey, procrastinated giving a response by taking a long swig. Lucy was about ready to slap the glass away from Lafitte's mouth, and Sebastian was about ready to punch Lafitte in the nose with the length of time it took him to give a yes or no to this simple question. Finally, Lafitte pursed his lips, "There is something you need to know Lucy. The truth is…"

Before Lafitte could finish his sentence, the tavern door crashed open, breaking the trance surrounding Lafitte's captive audience and silencing the rest of the pub's celebrating clientele. Lucy wanted to kill whoever had interrupted their conversation. It seemed as though Lafitte was on the verge of telling her some vital piece of information about Rackham and Anne. To her surprise, Gracie appeared in the doorway. She was being shoved by a snarling man with a scar across his left eye. *Bonny*! A knife was held firmly in his hand, poking at Gracie's back.

Lucy suddenly became aware that she hadn't even noticed Gracie disappear; she had been so wrapped up in her own thoughts. *How could she not have noticed that her only friend had disappeared?* She felt ashamed. That neglect was coming back to haunt both of them.

"*J'suis désolée*, Lucy," Gracie stated without any expression.

"I see 'ere some of me ol' friends," snarled Bonny. "It looks as though Anne's daughter 'az takin up with pirates, whorin' 'erself off jus as 'er mother."

Sebastian stood up abruptly, causing his chair to fall backwards and land with a crash. Silas and Seamus reached for their cutlasses.

"I'd be very careful about slandering the name of this woman," Sebastian hurled back at Bonny with his best captain's voice.

"Oh, I 'ave jus cause. Conspiring with pirates ain't takin lightly round 'ere. I watched ye disembark with this lot. The Governor, bless 'im, were very interested. An it also seems this gurl 'as 'elped this 'ere slave escape, another criminal action," Bonny sneered these offenses with obvious glee. "We can't allow the criminal element ta go unpunished, now can we?"

"You're a despicable liar. I have committed no acts of piracy. These gentlemen were kind enough to give me safe passage to New Providence; that is all. As for Gracie, she is my lady's maid and companion. If you have quarrel with her, you have quarrel with me Bonny. Release her, as she is a free woman." Lucy stood up and approached her accuser. Lafitte made an attempt to grab her hand and pull her back to safety, but she threw him off.

"She be not free, as she's the slut who spilled the fish on me good boots. I didn't get ta finish 'er punishment. The authorities are on their way ta arrest ye an send this one back."

Meanwhile, Gracie was rapidly cursing Bonny's name in French. "*Sale encule. Je vais te tuer. Pauvre naze.*"

Bonny had to pause in his monologue. "Shut yer trap slave!" The knife pressed more viciously into Gracie's back, silencing the girl. He turned his attention back to Lucy. "You should 'ave kept a better eye on yer gurl. I found 'er wanderin' round Merchant Row. It were easy ta nab 'er and 'ave 'er lead me right ta ye. Blame 'er if ya be blamin' anyone."

Bonny was becoming downright giddy in his triumph, which seemed to illuminate his ghastly scar even further. His glee only grew as a clomping of boots on cobblestones grew louder and closer to the inn. Shortly, a cluster of six soldiers in bright red uniforms, with bayonets held across their chests, appeared at the door. "We are under orders from Governor Rogers to arrest the runaway and Lucy Cormac on suspicion of piracy and aiding and

94

abetting a runaway slave," the captain of the guard stated flatly. "Stand down and turn over the criminals, or you'll all be arrested and hung."

Sebastian's hand automatically went to the cutlass at his side. Lucy, seeing this motion and fearing for his life, surrendered herself to the soldiers. "If you leave these gentlemen be, Gracie and I will come quietly."

"You can't give yourself up Lucy," Sebastian pleaded.

Lucy could see the urge to fight in the faces of Sebastian, Lafitte, Seamus, and Silas. "Let us go. We are at the disadvantage, at least for the moment."

The guards bound Lucy and Gracie's hands and led them out of the inn full of pirates. All looked on with amazement that of all the people in the establishment, two innocent women had been escorted out by armed guards.

Chapter 13

Fort Nassau Jail

Lucy and Gracie were taken to the Nassau jail, a shabby section of Fort Nassau built of solid gray stone, with a fetid stench of bodily fluids and dank cold hanging in the air. It housed six square cells with straw bedding and thick, iron bars covering doors and windows alike.

Gracie stood in front of their one, barred window and looked out on the soldiers completing their routine of daily drills in the garrison that lay below the jail. Her head leaned on the bars as she watched freedom happening outside. Lucy had shoved her body into a dark corner of the cell and remained motionless there, staring at the ceiling. She was in a state of shock. Events had transpired rapidly, and now she was under arrest for conspiring with pirates, which held a death sentence if she was convicted in court. She had been so close to learning something new about her parents; to be cut short in this search now was unfathomable. She was angry—angry at Bonny for being the spiteful scum that he was and angry at Gracie for being captured by him. Thinking about Gracie brought Lucy back to the present.

"Gracie, why were you snooping around Merchant Row unaccompanied? You just disappeared." As she started to emerge from her shock, her irritation at their joint entrapment grew. "You're a runaway. You knew how in danger you were. And now we both are in prison because you got caught."

Gracie lingered at the window, still watching the soldiers below. Lucy wasn't sure if her words had been heard, but Gracie's own annoyance was growing with every one of Lucy's words.

"You didn't even know that I had left, so why should I care that you're inconvenienced now? You aren't the only one with concerns."

"What concerns could you possibly have in Nassau that could be so important to risk being sent back to Martinique?"

A palpable silence followed this query. Lucy wasn't sure if her cellmate was ignoring her, but Gracie was debating whether or not the truth was worth telling. She wasn't sure she trusted Lucy at present. But they were both trapped behind bars, mostly due to her own actions. The options for their future weren't looking too hopeful, so there wasn't much to lose at this point. Gracie began her confession in such a low whisper that Lucy strained to hear her.

"I was looking for my brother."

"Your brother? In the markets?"

"I think he was sold to a merchant here on New Providence. He is thirteen now."

"How do you know he's here?"

"Word of mouth. Rumors spread amongst the slaves, from one island to another. It's the only way we can find out about family members. In the markets back on Martinique, every morning, I went to buy goods for the plantation owner; I tried to find slaves or freed slaves who worked on the ships. I told several men my name and my story and told them about my brother, what his name was, his family and his age. About two months ago, a message came back. A freed man on a merchant clipper came to port from New Providence. His captain had recently done business with a sugar exporter who had a boy of Shiloh's description sweeping floors and book keeping. The boy even knew my name." Gracie trailed off, tears coming to her eyes.

"That is why you snuck off then, to find your brother?"

"Yes...and to free him."

"That's impossible. How do you expect to do that?"

"I don't know, but I vowed that we would be together again. We have no one now but each other."

Lucy nodded her head in understanding. She too knew the loneliness of missing family. "What happened to your people Gracie?"

Gracie covered her face with her hands, and for the first time, let out a painful cry and sobbed as if she had never sobbed before. No one had ever asked her that question before. No one had ever cared. Lucy reached out her hand to Gracie in sympathy for her grief. She pulled the girl down beside her. After a while, Gracie quieted. When there were no more tears to shed, Lucy continued to hold her; and Gracie began to recount the events that had led her to this moment.

"My parents were brought from the west coast of Africa. They both were young and strong; so they survived the middle passage together. Many of the others didn't survive, including most of their family members. When they finally arrived on Martinique, they happened to both be sold at auction to the same sugar plantation owner, Monsieur Toulouse. Because they had been through so much together, they clung to each other for support. The Master gave them the names Felice and Bernard. They were both put to work in the sugar fields, working twelve hours a day in the hot sun. After a few years, my mother gave birth to me, and the Mistress put her in the house to do the washing and cooking. It was an easier job for a mother caring for a baby than the fields. When I was three, my brother Shiloh was born. I watched and played with him while my mother worked in the kitchen preparing meals for the Master's family. By the time I was five, I was helping with the cooking. Life wasn't too bad back

99

then. Even though we were slaves, we at least were together. I was able to spend the entire day with my mother and brother. I saw my father at night.

"My father's days were a lot harder though. I didn't understand or know how hard it was for him at the time. He and the field workers would come back to the slave quarters from the sugar fields at dusk, eat, go to sleep, wake long before sunrise, eat and then return to the fields. He did this same routine for thirteen years. Eventually the long, hot, hard days in the fields wore him out. He came in one night especially tired, so exhausted he could barely pat me on the head. He didn't even have the energy to eat. My father didn't wake up the next morning." Gracie paused, overcome by her memories and the loss of her father.

Lucy squeezed her friend's shoulder comfortingly. She could only imagine the pain of knowing and then losing a parent. "How old were you Gracie?"

"Ten years old," Gracie replied stonily.

Lucy wasn't sure if Gracie would want to go on, but she encouraged a continuation. "What happened to your mother and brother after that?"

Gracie turned dark, cold eyes to Lucy and then picked up her story again. "My mother was devastated, but she had Shiloh and me to care for still. So we went on, at least until a hurricane ripped through the island, destroying a year's worth of sugar harvest. The plantation lost a lot of money, so the Master decided to sell some of his slaves to make it through to the next harvest. My brother was nine years old. A good age for a slave auction. A new master could raise and train him and still get a lifetime of work out of him. So Shiloh went to auction. It was only recently that I found out he was bought by a merchant here on New Providence. The day Shiloh was taken away was far worse than when my father died. I helped raise Shiloh and had spent every day with him for nine years. It took three men to rip us apart. My mother cried for days. I couldn't comfort her. She was so upset that she barely noticed me anymore. Shiloh, her baby, might as well have died." Gracie wiped a stray tear from her eye.

"My mother revolted against the Master and Mistress in the only ways she could. She had control of the washing and the cooking. Every time she did the washing, one of the Master's favorite shirts would disappear, or the Mistress's best dress would mysteriously end up with a hole before an important social engagement. During dinner parties, the guests couldn't understand why the soup tasted of vinegar or the cake was salty instead of sweet. My mother was punished for these 'mistakes,' but a few lashes weren't enough for her to stop. This went on for about a year.

"But when Mother was whipped especially harshly when rotten fish was served to a potential wealthy suitor for the daughter of the household, my mother never recovered. It's not that she couldn't. She was still strong and could have recovered, but she didn't want to. She just let herself slip away; she gave up. I nursed her wounds for five days. She made me promise that I would search for my brother, and then she was gone. I was completely alone for the first time in my life. I was thirteen years old. Three years later I finally heard news of Shiloh and then met you. It was time to fulfill the promise to my mother."

Both women huddled together in silence. Gracie couldn't make the images of her lost loved ones disappear, and Lucy sat stunned at the suffering Gracie had experienced in her young life. Whatever had happened in Lucy's life was nothing in comparison to Gracie's suffering. It was far worse to have family taken away than to have never known the loss. She had at least grown up surrounded by people who cared deeply for her. Up until this point, everything had been about her own affairs. Maybe she would never find her mother; she already knew Rackham was gone forever, but there was hope for Gracie to be reunited with her brother. At least one of them had a family. "Gracie, I will help you fulfill that promise."

"Of course we have to get out of here first," Gracie reminded them of their sorry state. "I don't understand why that hideous man can't let what happened at the market go. I'm sorry I led him back to you."

102

"Yes, I believe that is actually my fault more than yours." Lucy realized her blame had been misplaced; Bonny wouldn't have bothered with Gracie except to get to her.

Gracie looked askance at her companion.

"That man is James Bonny. He hates me because he hates Anne Bonny, his former wife. She betrayed him decades ago and he won't let it go. That's why we're here, not because of you, but because of me. I am so sorry you were put in the middle of his plot for revenge."

"My actions gave him reason to have us arrested. That's why we're here now."

In the dimming light of the setting sun, the reality of their circumstances grew more hopeless. The two women contemplated their fates in a gloomy silence.

Chapter 14

Sebastian stood at the entrance to the stately white home of Governor Woodes Rogers. The gardens around the house were still impeccably maintained by the staff, and the white wash was still kept fresh. He hadn't stood in that spot in about seven years. The last time he had seen this house he was angry and swore he'd never be back, but now his presence was necessary to protect Lucy and Gracie.

At the sight of the soldiers leading Lucy away, he wanted to attack; it was a natural reaction for him upon seeing soldiers. He was tempted to draw his sword, but Lucy had stayed his hand. And she was right; nothing good would have come of going on the defensive at that moment. Sebastian wasn't usually the gallant type, coming to the rescue of damsels in distress, but he found himself intrigued by Lucy's passion and determination—risking life, limb, and reputation to find her parents. She had more guts than any other well-mannered woman he had ever met. Her eyes and comely form had an effect on him as well. He reminded himself that a great injustice had also taken place. Lucy wasn't a pirate—a stowaway yes—but not a pirate. It was only by accident that she ended up on the *Peril*; that was not deserving of the gallows. This thought sent shivers down Sebastian's spine and reaffirmed his mission.

He willed his boots to mount the stone steps, summoned his fingers to grip the knocker on the grand white door, and rapped three times. Within seconds, the door opened wide, and the visitor was greeted by a butler in smart black livery, accented with silver buttons on the cuffs. His long gray hair was tied back in a bow. The wrinkles masked the identity of this servant from Sebastian on first inspection, but slowly recognition dawned on him, as the wrinkles melted away into a familiar smile.

"Master Sebastian! Oh good Lord. Can it really be you? We heard no word of your return."

"Reginald, with you here at the door, it feels as though I never left. It is good to see you again. Have the years been kind?"

"As you can see, the years have come, but they haven't been too bad. Please, come in sir."

"No need for sir or master anymore Reginald." Sebastian took one last glance at the outside world and the fresh morning glow, before entering the Governor's Mansion and turning back time.

"As you can see sir, everything is as it was years ago. Even your room has been left the same. Will you be staying there sir? I will summon Nell to open the windows and dust."

"There is no need Reginald. I won't be staying any longer than is necessary." The hall echoed with their footsteps. Paintings and tapestries hung in the same places as his memories dictated. Young maids he no longer recognized flitted from room to room with dusters and rug beaters, just as they had in his youth.

"I assume you want to meet with the Governor, sir?"

"That is correct. Is he in his study?"

"Of course. It is nine o'clock."

"I suppose not much *has* changed here." Sebastian followed Reginald until they reached a thick door that was opened just a crack. Reginald knocked and then opened it further, announcing the presence of Mr. Sebastian. The man seated at his desk, immersed in documents and maps, dropped his pen; his gray eyes slowly moved from his writings to his butler in disbelief at the man's unprecedented intrusion on his office hours. Sebastian moved within the door frame, his hat in his hand.

"Hello father."

The Governor remained motionless, a statue of a sixty year old officer. "I see I've startled you and interrupted your work, but I come here on urgent business."

"You return after seven years to seek help." Rogers spoke his words slowly, without emotion. "How dare you enter this house, this respectable house. You, a deserter, a traitor to the crown and your father. I should have you arrested."

"As this house hasn't changed, so haven't you." Sebastian's temper began to rise. "I don't come for myself, but for another, an innocent woman."

"One of your crew? I doubt she's innocent."

"Do you know of whom I speak sir?"

"Lucy Cormac, the daughter of Anne Bonny and her runaway slave, Gracie. Aye, I know; James Bonny has told me everything I need to know. One of Anne's blood cannot be innocent."

"You know nothing of what you speak. She asked for safe passage on our ship. She did not take part in any acts of piracy. She was on board for two weeks. My crew overcame the vessel she and Gracie were aboard and scavenged supplies. Lucy... Miss Cormac and her servant opted to go with us."

"Why would an innocent woman choose to join your crew?"

"Some of my men knew her mother. She is trying to locate this woman."

"So she joins a band of pirates and helps a runaway. I see no issue here. Miss Cormac will be brought to trial and a judge and jury will decide her fate. I have work to complete, so I would ask that you leave."

Rogers went back to his papers, dismissing his son. He had for years wanted to see Sebastian again, had even left his son's room intact as a holy shrine, but at the sight of his son, he returned to the anger of years past. Sebastian remained in the middle of the room. This conversation was far from over. He still had two tactics up his sleeve if reason failed.

"Sir, I will not go. I have here a certificate stating that Gracie is a free citizen of the colonies." Sebastian pulled the official document out of his coat pocket, approaching the desk he threw it down in front of his father where he could not ignore it. The document had cost a good bit of silver, and fortunately, through allies on the seedier side of life, he was able to have the document forged by one of the best in the business. No one, not even the governor could dispute the authenticity of the paper. Clearly stated in an elegant print it read:

By the Authority of the Governor of the colony of Bermuda it is proclaimed that GRACIE LATOUCHE IS A FREE CITIZEN OF THE BRITISH COLONIES. March 5th 1737.

Rogers took the document in his hands and inspected it, taking his time. He finished reading and looked up at Sebastian, poised to speak, but before he had a chance, Sebastian continued. "As for your other charge against Miss Cormac—that of piracy, of which she is entirely innocent—you give me no choice but to use the threat you know I have the power to wield."

The Governor looked gravely at the young man and shifted uncomfortably in his chair.

"I will condemn myself to the gallows, confessing my crimes and life of piracy and inform the entire colony that the son of the Governor has not only left the British Navy, but become the captain of a pirate ship, sacking many of the crown's own vessels. This all being done with the full knowledge and, I dare say, protection of the Governor of the Bahamas." Sebastian had been fully aware for years that his father knew of his doings, and the only reason he hadn't been arrested was to protect the Rogers's name. The soldiers hadn't even looked twice at him when they had come for Lucy and Gracie, and he was a known pirate captain. As far as anyone else knew, Sebastian Rogers was still on board a British Naval ship. This bastion of civil order and crown law could never live with the shame of his son being a known traitor and scallywag.

Governor Rogers glared at Sebastian. How could his own flesh and blood besmirch his good name, a name he had cultivated and promoted as a well decorated admiral in the wars against the Spanish in the War of Spanish Succession and then again as a respected governor in the colonies, a position that had been a gift from King George I himself for his tireless service to the crown. But Sebastian was right, he would never risk that name and reputation. He had covered up his son's doings for years.

The Governor replied icily, "Miss Cormac and Gracie will be set free, but you and your crew will leave by midnight tomorrow and never set foot on these shores again, or I assure you, sir, my overlooking will not continue."

"That is fine Governor. I would expect nothing less from you."

Sebastian turned to leave, but before he reached the door, Rogers continued, "There is one other condition to this release. I want to see this Lucy Cormac. Send her to me."

"Why do you wish to see her?"

"That's my business," Rogers picked up his papers and continued signing and amending actions for the welfare of the colonies. "Good luck to you son."

Sebastian had barely heard this wish. His hand was on the doorknob. "Thank you father. I wish you well too." Sebastian opened the door and walked out, expecting to never see his father again in this lifetime.

Chapter 15

Lucy and Gracie were huddled together on the floor of their cell, comforting each other as they continued to discuss the sorrows of the past. They had spent three days in the jail, long enough to have acquired the stench of the prison. Their clothes were smudged, their hair unwashed and un-groomed. Still they had heard nothing. No one had visited. They seemed to have been forgotten. *But really who would care that they were there?* Lucy reasoned. The men she had recently met were just acquaintances, more interested in pillaging than her well-being. Sister Regina didn't know where she was. Sister Regina... she was so far away, and they had parted badly. *How could I have said those awful, hateful things to Sister after all she has done for me?* Lucy felt so ashamed that she had acted like such a spoiled child. If she could see one person in this world again, it would be Sister.

And then Lucy's thoughts turned to Sebastian. She had begun to think he cared for her, but that couldn't be the case. He had only helped her as long as it was convenient. Now his life would be endangered. She grew angry with herself for forming an attachment to him and even angrier with Sebastian for not caring. If she ever saw him again, he would rue the day. Her mind became cloudy with all forms of punishment. Really, his only crime was dancing with Lucy, but that was enough for her.

Just as Lucy was imagining herself forcing Sebastian to walk the plank at sword point for the tenth time, a stream of sunlight highlighted a few words that she hadn't noticed before scribbled on the wall. Now they glared at her, a message from the past. She wasn't sure if she was imagining it or not. She read the words aloud. *"Your walls couldn't hold my spirit—Anne Bonny."*

"What did you say?" Gracie asked groggily. She was just starting to nod off.

"Look, on the wall. Is it possible? It's a message from my mother. She was imprisoned in here." Lucy pointed at the illuminated words.

"Mon Dieu, c'est impossible." Gracie was now fully awake.

Lucy shook off her disbelief and slowly approached the words. She traced her finger over each precious letter, just as her mother had scrawled the letters years earlier.

Gracie's ears were the first to detect the clack-clack of boots approaching the cell. A red-coated soldier pulled out his ring of keys and opened the lock with a click. "Miss Lucy Cormac and her maid Gracie Latouche are free to go by order of the Governor of the Bahamas," the emotionless soldier reported. Neither Lucy nor Gracie made a move. Gracie didn't understand the English words, and Lucy was still imagining the woman who had written the message on the wall. The officer repeated, "Ladies, you are free to leave."

Gracie yelled at Lucy in French. "What is he saying?"

Lucy jolted back to the present. Realizing they were free to leave, Lucy grabbed Gracie's hand, and they moved quickly to the cell door, half expecting the announcement to be a joke. Lucy took one last glance at the words on the wall.

"Your escort is in the courtyard."

"Our escort?" Lucy questioned.

The guards led the two women down the single dark passageway to the large, heavy door that led to the world outside. The jailer once again produced his set of keys and clicked the lock. The door creaked open with great effort, and light glimmered through; fresh air engulfed Lucy and Gracie, their lungs filling with the purified scents. They gulped in the air, making up for days of putrid oxygen.

"You are free to go," the soldier encouraged.

Lucy and Gracie stepped into the sunshine. There, walking towards them at a quick pace was Sebastian. After cursing his name, Lucy had been so set against him, but instead of pummeling him, she threw herself into his arms, burying her face in his shoulder. Relief overwhelmed her—relief to be free, as well as to see this pirate again.

Sebastian embraced Lucy, pressing her against him, at once amazed and overjoyed at this expression of emotion. His left hand moved to her dark curls and stroked the soft hair; he nestled his head in her neck, feeling her soft skin against his cheek. "You don't smell so sweet," he reported in a soft voice, not bothered enough to pull away from the smell.

Lucy laughed into his shoulder. She pulled him closer. "I must smell foul," she giggled.

"Luckily, I'm used to the stench of men at sea. Compared to them, you smell like a rose." He laughed quietly and nuzzled her closer.

When the flood of relief finally passed, Lucy remembered where she was, realized Gracie was standing silently by as she made a scene. She pulled abruptly away from Sebastian's body. Their eyes met. "I'm sorry that I threw myself at you," Lucy apologized. She blushed slightly with embarrassment at her actions, but her eyes and voice remained steady.

"I'm not."

Lucy continued hastily. "I thought you had left us to rot. I was devising methods of torture if we ever saw you again." Lucy paused in her jesting. The real question dawned on her. "Why were we released?"

"That was my doing," Sebastian sheepishly confirmed.

"How? I can't imagine that you associate with the British government too often." Lucy was suddenly very curious.

"Let's just say that I have connections and leave it at that. We both know you are innocent of piracy, so you shouldn't have been arrested in the first place." Sebastian turned from Lucy and spoke to Gracie. "As for you Gracie, keep this document on you at all times." Sebastian pulled the certificate of citizenry out of his breast pocket and handed it to the girl. Lucy translated it from English to French.

"Gracie, you're free! How?" Lucy was overcome with excitement for her friend.

"Connections," Sebastian answered again. "I owed you for Silas's life. I promised you protection."

Gracie inspected the document; a wide smile of disbelief bloomed on her face. Even though she couldn't read it, the gold seal meant freedom. With the first real spark of hope entering her soul since her mother's death, Gracie wrapped her arms around Sebastian's waist. *"Merci, merci monsieur."*

Sebastian too felt true joy, both for Gracie's freedom and Lucy's gratitude for his service. It was rewarding to play the hero for a change, but he hid his pleasure behind glibness. "Two women throwing themselves at me in one afternoon. Who says the life of a pirate doesn't pay?"

Chapter 16

Lucy squeaked down the stairs into the heart of the Rooster's Crow after washing the scent of prison away and changing into a lovely lavender frock that Lafitte had laid out for her. It had been several hours since Sebastian returned the conquering hero to the tavern with the two thankful, rescued women. Silas and Seamus were incredulous of the fact that the Governor himself had issued a pardon. This was unprecedented, as the Governor wasn't known for his leniency. The duo was now, more than ever, impressed with the abilities of their leader. There was much hugging and happy greetings exchanged amongst the party at the Rooster's Crow upon their arrival. Relief for their freedom and the joy of being reunited with friends faded into a deep desire to attend to more bodily needs—bathing and eating. Lafitte set to work in the kitchen preparing a feast, while the women washed the last three days away.

Feeling now refreshed, Lucy found a late lunch set out on the table and Lafitte, Silas, and Seamus engrossed in conversation at the bar with a strange woman. Sebastian and Gracie were seated apart from the group, devouring plates of boiled potatoes, fish stew, and toast slathered in butter. Seeing the enticing repast, Lucy's stomach remembered that it hadn't partaken of a decent meal in days. But everyone in the room was so engrossed in their various activities that none of them even noticed her arrival, until Lucy yelled out, "Good afternoon. Could I get a plate?"

All eyes turned towards Lucy. Lafitte twitched uncomfortably, his eyes moving nervously from the stranger to Lucy. Silas and Seamus tried to avoid Lucy's eyes altogether. Gracie just kept eating. Sebastian went to the kitchen.

The strange woman had her yellow hair tightly wrapped in a bun. She wore a simple beige frock that hung off her body, ill fitting to her seemingly slender figure. The stranger focused on Lucy. *"Bonjour ma fille."*

The voice was familiar, so familiar to Lucy. A voice that had lulled her to sleep on many occasions, read to her, told her stories, and most recently had refused to tell her any information about Anne Bonny.

"Sister Regina, is it you?" Lucy gawked at the woman. She had never seen Sister Regina in anything but her black and whites. She looked younger and prettier with her hair exposed, rather than covered with a habit. But how could she be here, in the Bahamas, at a bar, with Lafitte, with pirates?

"You were more stubborn than I gave you credit for Lucy. After you disappeared I could only imagine that you might wind up in New Providence looking for Anne. I was so worried about you. When I told the Mother Superior what had happened she insisted that I come find you."

"Sister, I've so missed you, and I'm very sorry for the things I said to you." Lucy cringed to think of the awful words she had spewed at Sister. "I hope that you can forgive me."

Sister rushed towards Lucy, embracing her in a motherly hug. "*Ma petite*, there is nothing to forgive."

"Lucy, there's something else, another reason that Sister Regina is here. That she would think to come here." Lafitte was speaking now with hesitation. "Sister is actually *my* sister." He uncomfortably laughed at his own words.

With her head still resting on Sister's shoulder, Lucy too began to laugh. "You can't be serious. That's a pretty good joke Lafitte."

Sister pulled away from Lucy just enough to look her straight in the face. "It's not a joke, my dear. I am Pierre's sister. Pierre raised me, and I worked here at the Rooster's Crow until I was sixteen; then I joined the convent. Shall we say I always had a stronger relationship with God than my dear Pierre?" Sister paused for this information to settle. "You are actually wearing one of my old dresses. It looks much prettier on you than it ever did on me."

While Lucy was processing Sister's words, Sebastian returned from the kitchen with a heaping plate of fish and potatoes. "So it wasn't a coincidence that Lucy grew up in that particular convent on Martinique, was it?"

"You presume correctly captain. We didn't want you to grow up alone, Lucy. I know this is all very surprising, but it's nothing compared to what we have yet to tell you." Sister led Lucy to a chair, and Sebastian placed the plate in front of her. Her appetite had disappeared though.

Sister began to pace, while rubbing her forehead. "We have all," she glanced at Lafitte, Silas, and Seamus in turn, "kept the secrets of the past hidden from you. We wanted to protect you, but your tenacity to dig into the past has proven dangerous and led you straight back to the life we tried to shelter you from. So the time has come for us to revisit this history." Sister stopped pacing and nodded to Silas and Seamus.

Silas had one request. "Lafitte, please, a round for everyone. I'll take a double shot of your best whiskey. And keep it coming my friend." Lafitte was more than happy to oblige. And even though the afternoon was drawing on, and his best customers would be on their way, he closed the bar to any interruption. And Silas began to open old wounds.

Chapter 17

England 1697-1716

Young Mary Read was an unusual girl; in fact, she was barely a girl, since she had been raised as a boy from the earliest age. Her mother had foregone all frills and opted for an entire wardrobe in male attire for her daughter. Money was the cause of this bizarre transformation, as only money could be the cause of something so odd. Mary had a grandmother, who had a fair bit of money, but she really only wanted to bestow it upon a male heir, so Mrs. Read made good on that condition by providing a male heir where there had previously been none. Little Mary became little Mark and dutifully doted on the grandmother that provided for the family. For you see, Mary's father had died at sea some years ago, as most men who went to sea perish there in one way or another. Without his financial support, the family surely would have been lost, except for Mary's sacrifice of her feminine persona.

Mary actually took very well to this life as a male. The clothes were more freeing; the rules were less strict for a little boy than for a little girl. Her younger sister had to come in from the garden to help prepare the cakes for tea rather than stay out and build forts with the other lads from the neighborhood, as Mary did day after day. She also received a much better education, from a private tutor; Mary's grandmother insisted every bright young lad should be privy to an education in order to make his way in the world.

But once the first fresh years of youth had passed and Mary turned eighteen, the city life did not fit with her growing need for adventure. As a man, she could really do anything she wanted, as long as it brought in enough money to meet her meager needs. Her mother at this point had married again and did not require Mary's financial help any longer, and Ana, the younger sister, had become so prissy and primped for the life she had been groomed for that Mary had no use for her and knew she would be taken care of by a wealthy husband by the age of seventeen. So her family had no monetary need of her anymore.

And then there was a more urgent problem that arose that finally settled Mary on her desire to leave London. Her most esteemed grandmother decided that Mary must take a wife to continue the family line. This generous matron would bestow on her only grandson a worthy sum that would keep him and his new bride in fine style for many years to come. She compiled a list of the most eligible candidates and began to hold interviews with their noble parents. Mary wasn't too interested in taking on a bride at this point in her life. (And let's not forget how very surprised the poor bride would be on her wedding night.) So Mary snuck out one evening with a pocketful of silver coins, headed to the port, and bought herself a conscript into the navy. The next week found Seaman Mark Read aboard the *HMS Brigadier,* sailing to the English colonies in the Americas.

Life on board the vessel was difficult, sleep was hard to come by, and food was at times scarce. The crew was a lusty bunch of young men, who never once had a clue that Mary was indeed a female. She drank as hard as they did, pulled the ropes as hard and fast as they could, played cards with more cunning than they ever would, and never once batted an eye at the dirty jokes bandied about at the expense of the fair female sex. Mary even joined in; creating elaborate tales of the girls Mark had left behind in London town, for she had quite an imagination and had often kept her grandmother happy with her vivid imaginings. The crew grew to respect this young man, and some even envied his escapades; however, they would never admit that but would only counter with more far fetched tales of their own conquests.

During these long days at sea, Mary became particular friends with a young and handsome ensign by the name of Robert Hewes. They spent hours on deck sharing stories of their childhoods and hopes for the future. Hewes came from a very poor background and joined the navy solely to provide for his sickly father and young brother. Mary, for the first time in her life, became enamored. Up until now, boys had always been her comrades, but she found herself daydreaming about Robert, not of sparring and wrestling or other masculine antics, but of kissing his firm lips, the feel of his hands on her hips, and the smell of his neck as she held him. But to admit this infatuation would mean revealing her tightly guarded secret. After weeks of torturous debate, Mary decided that she trusted Robert; she had to trust him or she would go crazy.

Robert was on kitchen duty, peeling potatoes in a tiny room only fit for one person. Its sole exposure to light was a small opening near the roof. In other words, there was no way for anyone to peer inside the room. Mary stole away from her job swabbing the deck, snuck to this little room, and threw open the door, startling poor Ensign Hewes out of his wits. His potato and knife clattered to the floor. Mary laughed at his expression, finding him even more darling than before.

"Robert, I'm desperately in love with you and can't bear to live without you any longer."

She spoke frantically and then tore at her shirt, until the buttons were undone, and then unwound the white cloth that had so tightly wrapped her bosom since puberty, releasing her feminine features to the extremely astonished Ensign Hewes. His shock slowly melted into wonder, and then to elation, and then to lust. No woman had so forwardly exposed herself to him before, and he was overjoyed to find that his feelings of attraction over the past months were indeed aimed at a woman after all. So Robert did what any sailor trapped in a dim room with a comely female who had professed her love for him would do and wrapped her firmly in his broad arms, pressed her forcefully against the door, and kissed her expertly on the mouth.

Of course, after their tussle in the dark, Hewes proposed marriage, for he was a gentleman; Mary accepted, and at their first port of call in Philadelphia, they were married. With her remaining money, Mary was able to purchase a discharge for Robert and provide a down payment on a little tavern in Philadelphia. The captain of the *Brigadier* was only too happy to discharge Mark Read after learning his true gender. It was very bad luck to have a woman on board. It was miracle enough that they hadn't been struck by calamity as of yet. The happy couple settled down and lived contentedly together for one year.

***

Silas stopped short in his storytelling and took several gulps of his drink to refresh his dry mouth. "Ah, that hits the spot."

"That's not it, is it?" Lucy grew concerned. "This is a beautiful story, and Mary Read sounds like a fascinating girl, but I don't see what it has to do with Anne Bonny or Captain Rackham."

Sister Regina looked troubled. "Be patient Lucy. All shall be revealed in time."

"While I quench my thirst, Seamus, would you be so kind as to continue with the next chapter of our drama?" Silas urged his friend. "I worry that our young lass here might crack me in the head if I take a break."

"Aye, she does look a bit peeved. It would warm my old heart to speak of Mary Read again. It's been far too long since I last spoke of her." Seamus leaned back in his chair and returned to Mary Read, a woman he had loved as a daughter.

Chapter 18

New Providence 1717

Before the first year of Mary's marriage came to a close,
Robert was dead. He had been mown down by a runaway carriage
on the way to the jeweler's for a present for his beloved wife.
Unfortunately, he never got there, and the only gift Mary received
was her husband in a wooden box. Mary was inconsolable for
weeks on end. They had been very happy together and planned on
having children. With Robert gone, she no longer wanted anything
to do with the tavern or her life in Philadelphia. Everything there
only reminded her of the future that she had wanted with Robert.
So she sold the business and, with the money, set off for the
colonies in the Caribbean.

Without Robert, she returned to the comfort of disguising
herself as Mark again. She figured it was a safer way to travel, and
she would more easily find work as a gentleman, than as a widow.
Maybe she would return to the sea? She heard that there were
many privateers in the Caribbean who might have need of sailors.

***

Mary arrived in New Providence. The ship she was on needed to resupply; she meant to continue on to Jamaica, but while wandering the docks, her fortunes changed again. A woman with fiery red hair, flowing wildly around her shoulders, dressed in free flowing pantaloons, approached her aggressively.

"Hello my pretty youth. You're a fine looking lad. You look as if you could use some breaking in," gibed Anne, who thought she was addressing a handsome young man fresh off a long journey at sea.

Mary thought she'd toy with this brazen female a bit before revealing her true identity. "I could show you a thing or two strumpet. This is truly a wonderful place where I am greeted by tarts when disembarking. There's nothing better than a good shag to get the land legs back." Mary winked and stroked her suitor's chin.

Anne slapped the hand away. "Strumpet, tart! How dare you! I'm second mate of the *Revenge* and I'll draw and quarter you myself, you scurvy dog."

Mary laughed. "I was only having a bit of fun. I have more in common with you than you may at first see." She winked knowingly.

Anne Bonny took a more discerning look over this youth, from head to toe. Recognition dawned on her face.

"Bloody hell! You aren't a man at all, but a woman. Hah! And I was determined to have you. You are very convincing and own just as saucy a tongue as I. I do believe you and I are of a like spirit. What brings you to this devil of a place in this guise?"

"I'm a sailor in search of a vessel. I was led to believe that the Caribbean offered many an opportunity for young entrepreneurs of the sea."

"A cross-dressing sailor with a sharp tongue?" Anne's face lit up. "You aren't mistaken. You have landed exactly where a woman of your nature may excel. Search no further; you will join my crew. We could use a sailor of your salt aboard."

Mary couldn't help but say yes. She was in need of the work, and the fact that another woman, who knew her secret, was part of the crew made the offer even more appealing.

"Call me Anne. What do they call you?"

"Mary Read."

And from that moment, Anne and Mary were joined at the hip. Where one was, the other was only a few steps away. This fast friendship was too much for Captain Rackham, believing Anne was having an affair with this pretty youth who had been introduced to him as Mark Read. Anne laughed off his jealousy, until Rackham summoned Mary to a duel to reclaim his honor. Neither wanting to kill the captain of her ship or die for the sake of her identity, Mary exposed her lie. She opened up her bum freezer and then her blouse and *exposed* her tightly bound secret. Rackham went quickly from jealous rage, to perplexed shock, to confused embarrassment, until he settled on the acceptance of a second woman serving on his crew.

For a while, it was only Anne and Rackham that were aware that Mary was indeed a female, but over time she became known for her valor in battle and as an integral member of the crew and she revealed her identity to her fellow sailors. At this point, they were so used to Anne Bonny's presence on board that another woman barely made a difference to them.

Mary and Anne became like sisters. They toyed with every handsome man, tormented the authorities, and caroused into the wee hours. They had New Providence and the seas surrounding it at their feet, loving every second. As their infamy grew, so did the reach of their fame.

This notoriety grew to such an extent that the government became inundated with tales of their exploits—pillaging, murdering, kidnapping. Governor Rogers cringed at every new story that reached his desk concerning these women and the crew of the *Revenge*. He knew that action was imminent. To truly make his mark as an authority in the Bahamas he would have to rid the colonies of these dangerous women. He would have order, at any cost. He would not be made a fool of by two women dressed in breeches.

Chapter 19

Noah Harwood was one of the quieter members of the *Revenge's*
crew. He had been a forced conscript to the vessel when
Rackham's pirate crew overtook a passenger ship en route from
London to Bermuda. Noah was a shipwright and adept at
shipboard carpentry. Rackham was in need of this particular skill
to mend his vessel after the ravages of a storm or the onslaught of a
battle, so the options given to Harwood were either death or join
Rackham's crew for two years. Noah opted for piracy.

Harwood kept to himself for the most part. Mary watched
him carefully for weeks as he repaired the deck or attended to the
railings. He was rather tall and slender, but muscular in the way
that all sailors were. His short-cropped, red curls were always
tousled, and his blue eyes often looked sad. He worked swiftly and
whistled Irish ballads that he remembered from his childhood. It
was while whistling that his eyes lightened and an impish dimple
appeared on his fair, freckled cheek. Seeing this lightness in his
disposition, Mary couldn't help but approach the lad. "Harwood,
that was a lovely tune you were whistling. It sounds familiar."

Noah looked down at his feet, unable to make eye contact and stuttered out a few words. "It w...w...were one me Mother sang to me...I d...d...don't remember the name." He shifted his feet uncomfortably.

"Can I help you with your labors? I'm pretty good with a hammer."

Noah shifted, rubbing his sweaty palms together in agitation. "If you w...w...wish." Mary sat beside him and picked up one of the spare hammers and a few nails. They sat there without speaking for the rest of the afternoon, only the rhythmic pounding of the hammers broke the silence. Their relationship continued in this manner for several days. Mary was typically more forthright in her affairs, but she sensed that those tactics would just scare a man of Noah's temperament away. She didn't want to frighten him; in fact, she hadn't felt this smitten with any man since her late husband. So she was content to sit with him in silence as they completed their work, at least for now.

The following week, Noah was repairing the crow's nest high above the deck of the ship. Mary called out his name and waved to him, which caused Noah to drop his hammer. This incident would not have been so unfortunate if the said hammer had not fallen on the foot of a seaman passing below. The incident was made more unfortunate by the fact that the before mentioned seaman was known for his temper. He was not unaccustomed to stabbing a drinking buddy in a drunken fit for making off-color comments about his sister. This chubby fellow, whose name was Cutthroat Phil (the name said it all), bellowed and cursed in agony as he pranced on one foot. "You barmy arsehole, I'll see ye drawn and quartered; you clumsy git. You mute bastard, I demands satisfaction for nearly cuttin' short me life. I call ye out to a duel."

Mary was horrified by this encounter, especially at the mentioning of the word duel. Noah rarely took part in actual battles. Mary was sure that in a duel, especially one against Cutthroat Phil, Noah would be killed instantly. Before Noah could stutter out a response to his calling out, Mary clocked Cutthroat Phil soundly in the nose. Blood spurted from the wound. Still hopping on his good foot, Cutthroat Phil began cursing again as he grabbed his nose in agony. "You 'orrible litt'l bitch."

"I call you out to a duel. As soon as we come in sight of land, which should be tomorrow, we take up our pistols," Mary screamed in the face of the belligerent man.

The crew by this time was all standing around watching this fantastic theatrical presentation, which brought a pause to the mundane daily tasks of life at sea. The outcome was more interesting than anyone could have imagined. Mary and Cutthroat Phil going head-to-head on a beach? Simon, seeing opportunity in this performance, started taking bets, mostly in favor of Mary. The crew had witnessed her fine aim on many occasions.

By midday of the following day, the entire crew spotted a piece of land. Excitement for the duel was building. The ship anchored several yards off the white sandy shores of the island. It was a quiet cove in the shape of a half moon. Shrubby green jungles flanked the shimmering sands.

Four small row boats, packed beyond capacity with spectators, rowed to the shores. Those who couldn't fit in the rowboats huddled on the bow of the *Revenge*, vying for the best vantage point to the afternoon's event.

Mary rode in the first rowboat with Anne, who would serve as her second, Captain Calico Jack, and Noah. Noah felt horribly guilty about how this had all turned out, but he was secretly glad that he himself did not have to fight the duel. He held Mary's hand in solidarity, the first sign of affection between them. Cutthroat Phil rode in the second boat with his second, Robert Red, the ship's quartermaster and his only friend, a man with an equally vicious temper. Simon opted to take a neutral third boat with the bets, which he later regretted since it meant rowing with Silas and Seamus, who blathered back and forth about the scientific variables concerning weather, weapons' mechanics, and anatomy in ascertaining which participant was more likely to win the day. Silas was actually trying to distract his dear friend, who was growing increasingly anxious for Mary's welfare. In fact, Seamus had nearly taken Mary's place in the duel, but was persuaded otherwise by a sharp tongue lashing from Mary herself. The only solution at this point was intellectual argument.

The small boats landed on the beach; the duelers and seconds congregated around Calico Jack, officiate of the duel and master of the pistols. The spectators formed two lines the length of the beach facing opposite each other—a sort of gauntlet for the proceedings. Mary and Cutthroat Phil lined up back-to-back, and Calico Jack handed them each a weapon.

"At the count of twenty you will both turn and fire. Whoever draws first blood is the winner. On your marks."

Anne gave her friend a look of reassurance and kissed her on the cheek for luck, but Mary didn't really need it that much. She looked and felt calm and collected. She was sure of her aim and speed, which could only be faster than the large man standing behind her.

Captain Rackham began his count off, "1, 2…" The duelers marched in opposite directions… "7, 8, 9…" The crowds cheered their favorite and jeered their chosen loser. "13, 14, 15…" Anticipation mounted, as shown by the increasingly boisterous audience. Calico Jack finished his count, "19, 20 and fire."

Mary and Cutthroat Phil reached their destinations and then pivoted towards the nemesis aiming for him or her at the other end of the gauntlet. Mary leveled her arm, cocked her weapon with a click, and breathed deeply as she squeezed the trigger. Two cracks rang out, one from either side of the beach. One found its mark; the other flew off course, missing the shoulder of its intended victim by several inches. Cutthroat Phil fell with a shriek of pain and landed with the full weight of his body on the sand; the metal ball sunk deep into his heart, killing him within seconds of it piercing his body.

The crowd gasped; those who had bet against Cutthroat Phil cheered, while those who had bet against Mary handed over their losses to Simon with groans. A few mourned his death, like Silas and Seamus, for they were never ones to take the fickleness of life lightly. But the mourning lasted only a short time. "Well done my girl," Seamus praised Mary with relief.

Anne rushed to Mary and hugged her about the shoulders. Noah rushed to her side, thanking the heavens for preserving the woman who had saved his own life. He picked her up and hugged Mary to his chest.

"Finally you touch me. It took a duel and a death to get you to touch me," Mary jested in joy.

"I owe you my p...p...pitiful life Mary. I p...p...promise I will touch you often. Um...ah...ah, I mean whenever you want me to touch you," he corrected himself, embarrassed at his forwardness. But from that point on, there *was* a lot more touching between Mary and Noah.

Chapter 20

Rooster's Crow 1738

Lucy had been listening attentively to this story, waiting at every second to hear more about Anne and Calico Jack, but Seamus continued on mostly about Mary Read and this Noah Harwood, who frankly she really didn't care too much about. She was becoming agitated and annoyed. Lucy squirmed in her hard backed chair, waiting for news of her family.

"The whole crew knew how much Mary loved that boy Noah. She would have done anything for him, even die for him. Aye, she was a brave and loyal one, she was. A finer woman no man has ever seen," interjected Silas.

"Aye, she was a bonny lass. So strong and noble. And Noah adored her in return. She was the only person that he ever talked to. He wouldn't open his mouth for more than a 'yes' or 'no' to anyone else. But he was a nice lad and a true craftsman," added Seamus.

Lafitte was busying himself with cleaning glasses behind the counter. "Noah was a cute young thing. So innocent and sweet. I could tease him awful; make him blush to the roots of his red hair." He laughed lightly.

Lucy exploded. "Just stop! All of you! Why will no one tell me once and for all where Anne is? You keep talking about Mary and Noah and Cutthroat Phil, everyone but the people I actually want to know about."

"Youth is so anxious," Lafitte lamented. He looked over at his sister who was just finishing translating the conversation into French for Gracie's benefit.

"Not tonight Lucy; it's grown late," Sister attempted to soothe. And she was right, the time had slipped away. The dark of night had crept in hours earlier.

Lucy was about to protest. "She's right. You have to meet his Excellency the Governor tomorrow morning; remember, it's a condition of your release," Sebastian begrudgingly mentioned.

"How could I forget that detail? And I can't deny that a night in a soft bed does sound wonderful right now. So we'll leave the past alone for tonight and start again tomorrow."

"Well then, if you will follow me ladies, I will show you to that soft bed of yours," beckoned Lafitte.

"I bid you all good night." Lucy reluctantly withdrew.

"*Bonne nuit*," Gracie echoed.

***

After Lucy and Gracie had gone up for the evening, Sebastian was preparing to turn in for the night himself, when he overheard Sister Regina conferring with Silas and Seamus.

"I fear she will suffer bitter disappointment tomorrow. This story does not end where she thinks it does."

Sebastian only heard sighs of agreement and began to fear himself what truths still lay ahead for Lucy.

Chapter 21

After a restless night in which she was visited by the images of Anne, Rackham, Mary, and Noah, and even the softness of the bed couldn't quiet her mind, Lucy entered the Governor's study, announced by Reginald. Sebastian walked her to the gate of the house but refused to go any further. She assumed that a pirate probably wouldn't be welcome in a governor's house.

The pepper haired gentleman was poised over his work. After he heard the door shut, he lifted his head and inspected the girl standing in the middle of the room. She was silently taking the scene in, especially him.

"I was told you wanted to see me Governor." Lucy was nervous about meeting with Governor Rogers, but she wasn't going to let him know that. Would her mother have quavered in front of this man? Still, she couldn't help but wonder why she had been summoned by the head of the colony's government. If he wasn't going to throw her back in prison, he was probably going to demand she inform on Sebastian and the crew of the *Peril*. She wouldn't do it, no matter if it meant the noose.

"Please sit, Miss Cormac," Rogers motioned to a chair set in front of his desk. So this was the child of the infamous Anne Bonny. Anne had been a thorn in his side for decades and the question of whether this child actually existed had nettled him for years. Here was the proof now sitting opposite him. He never expected the daughter of Anne Bonny to be sitting in his office for a chat. Lucy looked a little worn and tired, most likely from her prison stay, but she seemed very well-mannered—not like her mother.

"So the rumors were true. You really do exist," Rogers mumbled more to himself than to Lucy. "I suppose you are wondering why you are here?"

Lucy looked squarely at the Governor. "I cannot deny that you have perked my interest. It is not every day that I am summoned to the elegant mansion of a governor."

Rogers was amused. "Likewise, you perked my interest when Bonny came to me with information about the daughter of Anne Bonny. I had to see you for myself—see this mythic daughter of the infamous Anne Bonny."

Lucy's heart began to beat rapidly with the reference to Anne. Her voice caught when she spoke again. "You knew my mother?" This had never crossed her mind.

"Yes, unfortunately I did. I've been governor a long time. Anne Bonny was a constant problem in my early years. She and Mary Read. I never knew women who could be so…difficult."

There was a question that Lucy still had hovering in her mind that had gotten lost in the excitement of her release and the unexpected appearance of Sister Regina. "Then, sir, might you know how Anne ended up in your jail? She left a message on the wall in the same cell I was confined to."

Governor Rogers puffed out his chest a bit. "Aye, I was the one who put her there."

Chapter 22

New Providence 1720

James Bonny had become a familiar sight to Governor
Rogers, so he wasn't surprised when the man was announced to his
study early one afternoon. Rogers wasn't at all fond of this man,
he was obviously just out to make a few bob by selling out former
friends, but he needed Bonny for information to clear the island of
the renegade pirates. Bonny arrived as grimy and greasy as ever.
His health and grooming had deteriorated drastically since his wife
had left him.

"What brings you here Bonny? Are you running short on
funds again?" Rogers inquired gruffly.

"Sir, there be three pirates that 'ave takin' over the seas
from 'ere to the Carolinas. They'll be a bonny prize for ye sir.
They robbed five merchant ships a the crown last week. Ye canna
allow them to make a fool o' ye can ye, sir?"

The Governor didn't like to agree with this man, but, in this
case, he couldn't deny Bonny's words. Captain Calico Jack
Rackham, Anne Bonny, and the latest addition to their crew, and

Anne's best friend, Mary Read, were running rampant over the seas. Their audacity was only increasing. Most recently they had raided a ship headed for London with molasses specifically meant for King George, kidnapped the captain for a ransom, and killed the first mate and many of the crew. They were so crafty at out-maneuvering and hiding amongst the many cays of the islands that the navy could never catch them.

Rogers tapped the tip of his quill on the desk and lay back in his chair as he considered Bonny. "What do you propose?"

Bonny was visibly pleased at the encouragement. He approached closer to the desk. "I've 'eard the crew'll be leavin' from the west end tomarra. She'll be weighed down wi' a load a' flour, so they'll be movin' pretty slow. They'll be stoppin' in Jamaica."

"So you think we could catch them in between? How do you know all this Bonny? I'm not ordering a ship and soldiers on a wild goose chase."

Bonny was very pleased to be asked how he came by this important information. He rested his right hand on the Governor's desk and leaned in. "This boy Yagers was feelin' a might chatty after a good bit a whiskey at the ol' Rooster's Crow. I got a trustin' face, ye see." He let this fact sink in thoroughly and then continued with his plan. "Ye know there be many places for a ship to 'ide in the passage to Jamaica. Yur soldiers could 'ide in one of them coves." Bonny smirked knowingly.

Rogers cringed a bit. "Please remove your hands from my desk. And take this for your troubles." He pulled a sack of gold coins out of his drawer and tossed them to Bonny. "Now get out."

"Yur too kind, sir." Bonny snatched the sack and hurriedly left the room, his eyes large with the fun he could buy with his prize.

Governor Rogers ordered a battalion to embark immediately. They would hide in a cove en route to Jamaica and wait until the *Revenge* arrived with its unsuspecting crew. Rogers was feeling pretty satisfied with himself.

***

Rackham, Anne, and Mary boarded the *Revenge* early the next morning, happy with their cargo and sure of the prize it would bring in Jamaica. They had looted the flour from a sloop just off the coast of Bermuda. Flour was rather hard to come by in the Caribbean and always brought a good price.

The crew was excited because the sloop bearing the flour also had a store of whiskey of a high grade, which had also been seized, not for profit, but for thirst. The sailing to Jamaica was predicted to be smooth, as not a cloud sullied the sky, and the emerald sea was as calm as a lake. With a carefree sail ahead of them, Rackham gave the crew, and himself, leave to partake of the whiskey below decks.

Mary and Anne took a bit of the drink but opted to stay on deck and try their hand at throwing knives. After the thrill of knives had passed, Anne pulled out her fiddle and sawed out a lively tune for Mary to dance around the deck to. It was actually a nice change of pace to be left without the men. They felt free to leave their hardened exteriors for a few hours and giggle and play like young girls.

Mary twirled, holding up her pant legs like a ball gown. "Anne, faster, faster."

Anne obeyed with furious strokes on the instrument, stomping her foot with the rhythm of the music. Mary whirled around the deck like a girl without a care in the world. For that moment, it was like Anne and Mary were the only people on earth, at least until the music came to a screeching halt. A vessel suddenly emerged from behind a rocky outcropping and caught Anne's eye.

"Anne, why did you stop? You can't be tired."

"Mary, look off the starboard bow. That ship that just appeared. It's coming toward us at a fast clip. What are the flags?"

Mary caught the urgency in Anne's voice and turned to the predator. "It bears the Union Jack, Anne. Call the men. The British Navy is coming for us."

Anne ran to the opening leading to the bunks below deck. "Everyone up, up, up! We're under attack! Grab your pistols," she yelled. All she heard in response was loud singing and carousing. "You idiots, get your drunken asses up here!" Her anger was building, an attempt at masking her real fear at their situation. Anne marched down the steps and kicked the nearest drunks she could find with her foot. "Useless asses!" Simon was stumbling around, yelling randomly in an unidentifiable language. Silas and Seamus were nowhere to be found, probably passed out somewhere. She spotted Jack sleeping in a corner with his head slunk over his chest. Without hesitating, Anne cuffed his right ear, which only served to knock him out flat on the floor. Anne screamed, "Wake up you lout! We'll all hang!" Seeing that her lover and the entire crew were immobilized, she pulled cutlasses and pistols off the drunks and dashed back to the deck.

"Mary, we're on our own. They're all completely drunk and useless. Here, take these pistols."

"We're alone, against an entire battalion of soldiers?" The reality of their situation dawned on Mary. She hugged Anne tightly, "My bonny Anne, I love you."

"Mary, if we shouldn't survive this fight, you are the companion of my life." They both laughed nervously and then detached from each other, transforming into battle-hardened mercenaries. They picked up their weapons and steeled themselves to the coming battle, elbow to elbow.

Fate arrived quickly, as redcoats flooded the decks. Mary fired, striking a lieutenant in the arm. Anne engaged with an officer in a crashing of blades. With her free hand, she fired her pistols at any flash of red that caught her eye. Mary kept a pistol in each hand, picking off armed men at a rapid pace.

As the women fought like Amazons against the onslaught, a contingent of British soldiers went below deck and, with only a few shots, pulled out the drunken crew one by one, each with his hands tied behind his back. As they were brought out into the light, they were lined up and tied neck to neck with thick rope.

Mary and Anne fought on, but were growing weary. A group of redcoats moved in, encircling the Amazons with bayonets, trapping them. Mary and Anne clasped hands; finally seeing the captured crew, they dropped their weapons in defeat. Anne found Rackham with her eyes; his head was bent with liquor. The unquestioned terror of the *Revenge* had sputtered to an end.

Chapter 23

New Providence 1720

The trial against the crew of the *Revenge* arrived in Nassau several weeks after their capture. News had spread amongst all pirates in the area that the most infamous captain and women of the high seas were summoned to court and would inevitably be hung. Fear spread with this news. A lifestyle was dying with them.

The judge, in his fine, long, red robes and white wig set upon his wizened head, was seated in front of the small courtroom in the government building. The bailiff announced the trial of thirty-four members of a crew that had committed acts of piracy. He then announced the names of each criminal as they marched into the courtroom in a somber line. Beards and hair were straggly and dirty from weeks in prison. Their shirts were tattered and caked with muck. "Robbie McCary, Jack Rackham, Anne Bonny, Mary Read, Noah Harwood, and Simon Callow..." All in the somber procession had their hands shackled in front of them with unrelenting iron.

"You are all charged with murder, kidnapping, theft, blackmail, extortion, and piracy in the seas surrounding the islands of the Caribbean. Do you have anything to say for yourselves?" The judge looked on the crew before him with a blank expression. Many pirates had come up before him in the past ten years. They were guilty, no doubt. This was the usual assortment of ruthless, unkempt men who thought they could live outside of crown law that had come before him in the past... except for the two women at the end. Women who had taken to piracy were unusual. His stare paused on them for a good length of time. Even with their hands restrained, they linked fingers in solidarity. But unlike the men, they both looked him full in the face. "How do you plead to the charges against you?"

One by one, each member of the *Revenge* curtly replied, "Not guilty." It was all just as the judge expected. Then the judge turned to Anne for a reply.

"Your honor, I plead not guilty. Being quick with child, I pray that execution might be stayed."

And then the other one opened her mouth. "Your honor, I am not guilty of these charges. I too plead my belly."

Whispering amongst the bystanders in the court grew in volume at this unexpected drama. The judge hammered his gavel to silence the audience. He stared at the two women. Lying most definitely. There was no way they could have babies in their bellies. It was just a ploy to avoid the noose. But the law was the law; a baby could not be punished for its mother's sins.

"You plead your bellies? Both of you? Well, the court will appoint doctors to confirm your states."

Several witnesses were then brought out to speak of the atrocities committed by the pitiful creatures standing before the court. One man spoke of being kidnapped, another of his stores of brandy being stolen. A woman took the stand and pointed to Anne and Mary. "My canoe was overtaken, and my provisions were taken. These two so called women threatened me with their axes and pistols. They threatened to murder me if I spoke out against them. They wore men's jackets, long trousers, and handkerchiefs tied on their heads. I only knew them to be women due to their obviously large chests." The witness sneered at the pirates, tossed her head at them in defiance, and then stepped down.

A final witness was called, a Mr. James Bonny.

Bonny nearly pranced into the courtroom; he was obviously overjoyed now that fortunes had changed in his favor. "Aye, that there Captain Rackham plundered a shipment a flour from a merchant vessel and was a plannin' to sell it in Jamaica. He an 'is crew murdered five a the sailors. An that red headed one...," Bonny was pointing and glaring vehemently at Anne, "she be the worst a the bunch. She walked out on 'er weddin' vows an took up with this low-life Rackham. She's a 'arlot is what she is."

The courtroom was growing rowdy with Bonny's accusations. The judge banged his gavel and signaled for Bonny to leave the stand. As he departed, Bonny spit on Anne; luckily his aim was off and, instead of hitting her in the face, the spittle landed squarely on her boot. Anne stared daggers at him, imagining a gruesome death for this scum of the earth.

When the drama of Bonny dissipated, the judge turned back to the defendants sulking in front of him. "Upon hearing the evidence given by the witnesses, this court finds you all guilty of acts of piracy."

A rumbling began to boil in the courtroom.

The judge ignored the discontent and continued in his sentencing. "Anne Bonny and Mary Read, until your wombs are found to be vacant, you will be held in Nassau prison." He shifted his attention to the male members of the crew. "The rest of you have been found guilty by this court and will be hung from the gallows tomorrow at noon."

The rumbling in the court grew again at the pronouncement of the verdict. It wasn't unexpected, but the news of the pregnancies was worth gossiping about. Some in the court were more genuine in their feelings towards the approaching hanging.

Lafitte sat silently on a bench in the back of the courtroom with his hand covering his tear stained face. He had been in shock since first hearing that Rackham's crew had been arrested. It shouldn't have been so shocking. They were outlaws, and pirates were captured or killed almost inevitably, but it was a thought he always pushed away. But now, as he sat in court with the reality of losing so many friends, it didn't seem like life could possibly go on. Anne, Mary, Rackham, Noah, and, he could barely think the name…Simon. He couldn't think of a future that didn't include Simon in it. Lafitte lifted his grief stricken eyes and found his beloved's face. Simon weakly grinned and gave a quick wink to Lafitte. Lafitte blew a soft kiss back to him and then sat motionless, watching Simon until he vanished from the room. It would be the last time Lafitte would see Simon in this world. He wouldn't attend the hanging. He just couldn't bear to see Simon meet his fate. If Lafitte didn't see the end, he could believe that Simon just disappeared. He was somewhere off on the high seas, maybe returned to his native land.

Meanwhile, the lot of criminals was being escorted from the courthouse and across the yard towards the carts that would take them back to the jail in Fort Nassau.

"Ye bitch in britches, I tol' ye I'd get me revenge."

Bonny emerged from the shadows of the government building, nearly falling over himself with glee. "Life in prison. Too bad it's not ta be the noose. I'd 'ave lov'd to see ye strung by the neck. But you Rackham, this is what ye get, takin' a man's wife." The sneer on his face grew. He was so close to the group, the soldiers and the criminals.

Anne could see the pure joy of revenge in his eyes. Rage overpowered her. This creepy bastard would win after all. The guard in front of Anne had a short knife strapped to his side. She snatched it in one swift move and then sliced the smirking, puffy face in a deft motion from eyebrow to lip. Blood spurted from the fresh wound and Bonny fell in agony, cursing loudly. Several soldiers rushed to Anne and grappled the knife from her hands. A soldier slammed the butt of his musket into her side, but Anne wasn't cowed yet. "This isn't over Bonny. You'll rue the day you see my face again."

The soldiers pushed Anne and the rest of the crew away from the scene, while a few bystanders attended to the writhing, howling form on the ground.

Chapter 24

New Providence 1720

The execution of Rackham's crew dawned on a cloudy day.
A light drizzle shrouded the proceedings. Mary and Anne were
given permission to join the throngs in the courtyard of Fort
Nassau to witness the hanging—under armed guard of course.
Many from the island had gathered to bid adieu to these men, for
they weren't disliked. Many had been conscripted by the navy or
had turned to piracy to escape unfortunate circumstances, and most
importantly, they had increased the economic wealth of the island
through their less than honest means.

At ten minutes to noon, the crowd fell silent as the
condemned men were marched into the middle of the courtyard,
where an impromptu gallows towered over the crowd. On this
day, the hanging was the main event, and the gallows were made to
draw attention to the fate that awaits those who disobey the laws of
man.

Mary and Anne scanned the familiar faces: James, Big
John, Crabby Pete, and so on, as they made their way to the

gallows. Some still breathed the freshness of youth while others wore the accessories of old age. Some whispered prayers beneath their breaths to a God they hadn't known in years; others stared at the ground in silent fear of the moment to come; others staggered drunkenly to their doom after imbibing their last precious drams of rum.

Captain Calico Jack Rackham entered the courtyard, his eyes searching the crowd for Anne. Anne was waiting for a glimpse of her captain, and when she finally spotted the familiar calico suit, a little worse for wear, she stepped closer. "If you had fought like a man, you wouldn't be dying like a dog," she shouted at him, her eyes wide with grief.

The faint outline of a smile crossed Jack's face. "Vicious to the end. I'll wait for you on the other side my red-headed queen." His voice hushed.

Anne lunged clumsily and caught his lips with hers for one last time before she was forcibly hauled backwards by the guards. Calico Jack was pushed forward, his eyes locked on Anne's until the crowd closed his view.

Mary would have been touched by this woeful scene if she hadn't been distracted by her own grief. She watched as Noah Harwood brought up the rear of the sad procession. He was as handsome as ever, quiet eyes concentrated on his feet, hair tousled; his strong shoulders were more sagged than usual, but still

155

beautiful and strong. All others faded as Noah passed in front of her.

"I bury a second husband today, and I shall grieve as any widow for her beloved until my own death finds me," she whispered just loud enough for Noah's ears. Tears misted his eyes, and his mouth quivered as he tried to find the words for this most unique of women.

"I c...c...carry you into the next world, since this world has not g...g...given us enough time. Keep our child safe; it is all that remains of you and me and this life." He tried to reach out his bound hand, but was prodded by the bayonet at his back. Mary stood proudly until he disappeared and then buried her face in Anne's shoulder, sobbing for her loss.

The morbid proceedings began as a chaplain appeared on the gallows with the masked hangman. The spiritual leader spoke of meeting the maker, recognizing the authority of God and the courts, seeking repentance for a life of sin, and finding forgiveness in the afterlife. The convicted men were then organized; the first five victims climbed the scaffold to meet five thick ropes, the first sacrifices. The former pirates were each given a turn to say their last words and free their souls of any sins. The executioner then placed canvas sacks over the victims' faces. The beat of the snare drum thumped, and the ladders on which each man stood were twisted out from under their feet one by one. The audience witnessed the thrashing of legs and the convulsing of bodies, but the most horrific sight was considerately hidden from view under the canvass masks. The struggle for survival caused the faces of the condemned men to turn purple and tongues and eyes to bulge out of their heads, until silence finally removed all suffering. This sequence reoccurred twice more before Rackham, Simon, and Noah were brought to the ropes.

When his time came, Rackham spoke to the crowd with the command of a captain. "I regret no part of my life in this world. I have served with great men, all true and loyal. Together we have lived beyond the constraints that cage most men like animals. A pirate's life is the only life for a man with spirit. And, I die with the love of the most courageous of women in my heart, having had the pleasure of her company and fortitude through times of battle and peace." He looked squarely at Anne; her fiery hair would be his last glance on earth, the image he would carry into the next life.

Noah looked to the heavens and then shut his eyes to reality. "I die with hope that G...g...od almighty will be merciful to me. I ask his f...f...forgiveness for all my earthly sins."

Simon spoke next. "This life has been unfair. I hope the next will prove better. I was pulled to these shores against my will; I am guiltless of any crimes. Crimes were committed against me; I did what was necessary to regain my own self-respect and independence. An independence that is owed to all men, and

157

should be neither possible nor acceptable for another man to take." A fire had sparked within Simon. He spoke with a force and vehemence that no one had heard from his lips before. There was nothing left for him to lose in speaking the truth at this moment. And all ears were tuned to him for a change. "God will not judge me but those who have acted against my person."

With their last words, the hangman hid the criminals under canvas. The bag cut Anne's gaze from Rackham's stoic face. Mary remained sobbing on her shoulder, unable to watch the proceedings. "They are up Mary. The gallows are about to fall." In the next moment the thunk of the ladder came. Anne shuddered, and Mary let out a shriek of deep sorrow. The Golden Age of Piracy was dead.

Chapter 25

New Providence 1738

The Governor rose from his chair and stared out the window at the sailboats passing on the sea as he finished recounting his memories. His back was turned to Lucy.

"All hung…Rackham, Noah, and Simon. Poor Lafitte. He never said. Such a waste." Lucy wiped a few stray tears from her cheek. "What a horrible tragedy for Anne and Mary to witness. Sir, what happened to my mother?"

Rogers turned slowly, his hands clasped behind his back. "I don't know what happened to Anne. She disappeared. She left that note on her cell wall and escaped from the jail, supposedly with a baby. I guess that rumor was true," the Governor said wryly. "I've heard rumors over the years that Anne reunited with her father in the Carolinas. Others claim she took up with a merchant vessel crew out of Bermuda."

"She escaped prison with a baby?" A terrible sense of the circuitous nature of life hit Lucy. "So, you mean, that I was born in that prison, in the same jail cell that I was just held in?"

"It would seem so."

They both pondered this absurdity silently for a moment.

"Miss Cormac, I called you here because I was hoping you might be able to give me some insight into what happened to Anne Bonny. Her disappearance has nettled me for nearly twenty years. But I see now you are as clueless as I. I do however know what happened to Mary Read, if you are interested?"

"What?"

"She's buried on Sugar Hill." He pointed out the window to a hill that lay between the Governor's House and Fort Nassau, looking over the sea. "She died in her cell the night Anne escaped. Those two were never out of each other's company. It must have been a real blow to Anne."

Rogers straightened the white lace peeking out from under his cuffs and walked closer to Lucy. "Can I offer you some advice Miss Cormac?"

Lucy looked up at the Governor. "Of course."

"Do not follow in the footsteps of Anne Bonny or Mary Read. Stay away from certain influences that may lead you into that lifestyle. It leads to prison, hanging, or death by scurvy or the sword." He genuinely wanted to offer this girl advice he felt she needed. Without decent parents, who would guide her? "You were born in a prison cell, but you need not return to one."

Lucy rose. "Thank you sir for the fair warning. And thank you for sharing what information you have on Anne, but I must take my leave. I am expected back." Lucy stuck out her hand. Rogers extended his own and pressed the offered hand affectionately.

"Good luck to you Miss Cormac."

Lucy took her leave and closed the large door behind her. In the hall, Reginald met her. "I will escort you out Miss."

As she followed the aging butler down the stately hall towards the main entrance, Lucy admired the paintings on the wall. There was one in particular that grabbed her eye, the painting of a young man in the trappings of a British naval uniform. His long sandy hair was tied back from his face, his blue eyes alert and expectant. He was younger and better groomed than the man she knew, but it was, without doubt, Sebastian. "Excuse me. Who is this young man?"

Reginald lit up. "That is the Governor's son Sebastian Rogers. This was done several weeks before he took his place on his battleship. We were all so proud. He actually came by the house just yesterday. It was quite a surprise to all of us because we hadn't seen him in seven years. The navy keeps him out at sea."

"He is handsome in his uniform." Lucy took a last inspection of the man; a man that she had never met.

Chapter 26

Ambling down the long drive from the Governor's Mansion, Lucy spied the familiar, lanky form of Sebastian loitering on the other side of the gate. She was happy that she was returning to this version of Sebastian and not the one in the painting. Her Sebastian was a man free to live by his own rules; the painted version looked like a man constrained by the wishes of others. The man in front of her greeted her with a smile of contentment.

"How did it go with his Excellency?" He had been anxiously pacing, wondering why his father wanted to meet with Lucy, but now that he saw her again a calm spread over him.

"He wanted to warn me to stay away from the bad influence of pirates," she grinned at Sebastian and then continued more soberly. "He recounted how the crew of the *Revenge* was captured and hung. He was the one who ordered their capture. Anne and Mary ended up in prison, and Mary died there. But he, like everyone else, doesn't know what happened to Anne. She's like a ghost, just vanishing into thin air. The more I learn, the more I don't want to know. If Rackham truly is my father, he was hung to death in front of my mother. I had such a different image of my parents—that my father was some sort of heroic figure and my mother forced to give me up because she had no other choice. Not that my parents were imprisoned and my father and his companions hung like animals. I...I...," Lucy's voice broke as a lump of dread and doubt made its way up her throat.

Sebastian gently rested his hand on her shoulder. "I am sorry you aren't finding what you want Lucy. I wish I could help in some way, but parents don't always live up to our expectations. The only thing you can do is to find your own path in life."

The last comment broke Lucy's thoughts from the tragedies of the past and reminded her of another important discovery of the day. "You're the Governor's son." She paused for him to acknowledge this information, but instead of making any comment, he withdrew his hand and just looked at her, waiting. "You used your connection with the Governor to release Gracie and me, didn't you?"

Sebastian took a deep breath before beginning. "Yes, Governor Rogers is my father, which doesn't give me quite as much clout as you might think Lucy. He doesn't like me or the decisions I've made very much. In case you didn't know, he doesn't like buccaneers very much, especially ones in his own family."

"You call yourself 'Strongbow.'"

"My mother used to sing a tune about a hero named Strongbow. He roamed the Highlands of Scotland rescuing maidens in distress, righting the wrongs of the land, bringing the corrupt to justice—through his skill with a bow. My mother had a gorgeous voice. Alas, she died of tuberculosis when I was but five. When I took to the high seas, I didn't want any of my crewmates to know that I had any relation to the man responsible for destroying their way of life." A recognizable grin returned to his face. "And Strongbow sounded like a good piratical name. One to strike fear in the masses."

"But it's also a good name for a hero."

"Don't go romanticizing me, Lucy. I, like your parents, have committed crimes that are punishable."

"That may be true, but yesterday, you saved Gracie and me from prison, Sebastian. That's the act of a hero. In fact, what did you do to get us out?"

Sebastian met her intense stare. "Why do you need to know? Aren't you content to be free?"

"You haven't set foot in that house for seven years; the butler informed me so."

"This is true. Reginald was always fond of me, more so than Rogers ever was. But why do you care when I last visited the house of my father?"

Lucy now was becoming aggravated at Sebastian's avoidance of her inquiries with inquiries of his own. The timbre of her voice rose. "I'm curious why you took this opportunity to make your first attempt to reconcile with your father."

"I thought you wanted to know how I got you out, not why I visited my father?" Sebastian was enjoying this banter. He could see the annoyance growing in Lucy; it amused him, and he was finding it more and more difficult to keep a smile from sneaking to his lips.

Lucy turned her face away from Sebastian's view as they continued their slow meandering through the streets of Nassau. Her voice was calm when she spoke again. "I want to thank you for seeing your father to have us released. Whatever you did, it was probably not easy for you to enter that house again. I just don't understand why you would risk being captured after all these years?"

Sebastian stopped and turned abruptly so that he stood directly in Lucy's path, just inches from her person. "I did it for you Lucy. I wouldn't have gone back there for any other reason but for you." A lump formed in Lucy's throat as she listened in wonder. "I threatened to expose the horrible truth that the Governor's son is a buccaneer (in fact a pretty good buccaneer whom he's never attempted to arrest), thus destroying his good name."

Sebastian, seeing the soft wanting in Lucy's eyes, stopped explaining himself and placed his hands on Lucy's face, one on either side, pulled her lips closer and then crushed them with his own. Lucy lightly slipped her hands around Sebastian's back. She could feel the welts seared on his skin beneath the thin shirt. The feel of Sebastian's warm mouth had completely erased any other thought from Lucy, including the fact that they were standing in the middle of the street, right outside the Rooster's Crow.

Finally remembering herself, Lucy blushed slightly and pulled away from the moment, even though it was hard to force herself from the comfort of the gallant pirate before her. She giggled nervously, "Sebastian, they probably can see us through the window."

Sebastian nodded in agreement, reluctant as he was to return to reality. "Lucy, there was one other caveat to your release, besides your meeting with the Governor." He paused, "I must leave New Providence with my crew by midnight tonight and never return to these shores or the Governor will see me hang."

"You have to leave? But where will you go?"

"I don't know; probably return to the more southern islands. Wherever we can hide and attack, as we've always done."

"Will I see you again?" She said it so softly, afraid to ask the question.

In answer, Sebastian brushed a few stray curls from Lucy's face until his hand came to rest at her neck.

Lucy's mind quickly flashed from one possible future to another. She might never see him again. Sebastian could be killed in battle; captured, hung…She would lose him. That couldn't happen, not now. An idea began to swirl in her head. It sounded absurd in her head, but even more absurd when said aloud.

"I want to come with you, fight alongside you; be with you. I'm an orphan, a bastard, and a pirate's daughter, a triumvirate that makes me perfect for a pirate crew. I'll probably never find Anne Bonny; no one knows where she is. And if I do find Anne, I don't think I will like what I discover. I have no family, nowhere I belong. But I know I belong with you."

"Lucy, you aren't meant for piracy. It's a hard life, harder than you can imagine. I can't bring you with me and risk your life. It just wouldn't be right. You have your own life to lead."

"You're right; it is my life and my decision, and I choose you. As long as I am with you, it doesn't matter how difficult life is." Before Sebastian could resist again, Lucy stopped him. "Do you want to be with me?"

"The thought of leaving without you is unbearable."

"Well then, there's nothing left to discuss. I'm joining your crew. We leave tonight."

167

Sebastian lightly brushed his lips on Lucy's. He wasn't too excited that Lucy wanted to become a pirate, but he was overcome with joy that she wanted to be with him. Lucy's lips responded to the warmth of his and pulled him closer. Her hands clasped around Sebastian's bronzed neck, while his hands roamed to her waist and held her securely against his lanky body.

Chapter 27

Sebastian handed Lucy a sack of silver coins to purchase provisions for her journey and a dagger for protection in the rough streets of Nassau. He left a glowing Lucy still standing in front of the Rooster's Crow, while he returned to his ship to make preparations to leave by the stroke of twelve. She had promised to meet him back on the *Peril* after she said her goodbyes. Lucy was still in a daze when Gracie appeared out of nowhere.

"Lucy, *s'il vous plaît, mon frère*. I saw my brother," she cried urgently.

Lucy was suddenly pulled out of her happy musings. "Gracie, what's happened?"

"My brother. I was down by the wharf and saw him with a large man, with glasses, and a long gray beard. They were too far away. I lost them in the crowd and couldn't follow. Please, help me find my Shiloh! I can't lose him again."

While Lucy had been meeting with the Governor, Gracie, using the freedom granted to her by the official certificate procured by Sebastian, had returned to snooping around the docks. She spied a face that was so familiar and made her heart swell with sisterly love. Gracie tried to follow the boy, but he turned a corner and disappeared in the bustle of the crowd.

This was all hastily recounted by Gracie as she pulled Lucy along behind her.

***

Sister Regina, who had been watching Lucy's strange interactions from inside the Rooster's Crow for some time, now was surprised to see the two women sprinting off through the streets of Nassau.

***

Lucy and Gracie searched shop after shop in the merchants' quarter of Nassau, looking for a large man with a beard and glasses. They found tall, skinny men with white wigs; old, crippled men who smelled putrid; short, bald men with chronic runny noses, but no large men with gray beards and glasses.

As the hours slipped by, Lucy became anxious that she wouldn't get back to Sebastian in time for his departure, and Gracie began to fear that she had only imagined the vision of the morning. Each of their musings was interrupted by a screech emanating from across the cobble-stoned street. Scattered carts and horses somewhat obscured their view, but the perpetrator of the screech was a young woman in a bright yellow dress, fitted snuggly to her figure, accessorized by a matching yellow bonnet and parasol. "Over here, over here!" The yellow girl was frantically waving her hand at Lucy, beckoning her across the street. Lucy, with Gracie in tow, hesitantly crossed the street, avoiding the strategically arrayed soft, brown patties.

"Oh I knew I recognized you," the girl in yellow greeted Lucy. "You were on the ship with us out of Martinique, before it was attacked by pirates. They were so rough and strong, with their wild hair streaming down their backs..." She drifted off before brushing away her dreamy reminisces; she then continued more soberly, "I don't know who could ever be a pirate, let alone love a pirate?"

Lucy slowly began to place this odd person dressed like the sun. She was the eldest daughter in the gaggle of children who shielded Lucy as she stowed away on the *Queen Mary*. Lucy tried to ignore the sun princess's last comment. "I do remember you. How has your visit to New Providence been? You came to visit your uncle, right?"

"Oh, yes, we've had a wonderful time in Nassau. So many sailors running around the docks. Uncle Teddy isn't exactly a thrilling man, but he gives me a fine allowance for clothing." To accentuate the importance of this quality, the sun princess swooshed her dress back and forth, showing off the fabric's lightness.

171

As the three girls were standing on the street front, a largish man with a gray beard, glasses, and tufts of graying hair sprouting in a neat circle around a balding head waddled out onto the front stoop in front of the house marked Sampson's Shipping. "Celia, oh Celia, there you are dear, you're finally back. Tea is ready. We were just waiting on you dear." The large man was frantically waving at Celia in case his booming voice hadn't caught her attention.

"Oh, it's Uncle Teddy. He never misses mealtime, and no one else may either. He does make the most luscious lemon cakes though. Would you like to join us? We always have loads of extra, and I could use a reprieve from talk of shipping this and that to wherever." Celia so glowed with enthusiasm at this brainstorm that Lucy wasn't sure how she would turn the poor girl down.

"It's very kind of you, but we are very busy right now. We don't really have time to stop," Lucy kindly tried to turn Celia down.

Just as the glow in Celia's eyes was slipping away, Gracie nudged Lucy. Gracie leaned in so that only Lucy could hear her whisper. "Look through the window. You see the boy with the broom? That's Shiloh." Her voice caught.

Lucy's eyes wandered to the window and found a dark boy of about thirteen years of age sweeping the floor. "Celia, I've changed my mind. I do have some time and could use a rest. I would love to accept your offer of tea. We could catch up on all of our adventures since Martinique."

The glow returned to Celia's face. "Oh, wonderful," she screeched. "And your maid can go to the kitchen for a cup of tea," she said dismissively and pointed to the basement entrance to the house, reserved for slaves and servants.

Lucy was about to protest Celia's request, but before she could open her mouth, Gracie whispered, "Just go. Find my brother. I'll go to the kitchen." Lucy nodded and followed Celia up the stairs to the pink clapboard house, while Gracie descended the steps to the basement kitchen.

Upon entering the house, the two girls were greeted by three identically freckle-faced boys. "Celia, where have you been? We're hungry," they shrieked. Around the room several more children of all ages were running around, hitting each other, wrestling, throwing any objects that weren't nailed down, and screaming at the top of their lungs. Meanwhile, Uncle Teddy was pulling what little hair he had left out, running after the children, picking up fallen objects, and screaming at the top of his lungs. "Miranda, that's a very expensive vase; don't throw it at your brother. Denny, don't kick your sister Mary."

"They are a bit rambunctious, but they really can be sweet," Celia apologized for the chaos. "Okay children. It's teatime. Everyone, take your seats at the table," Celia called

173

cheerily. And, as if by magic, all the children ceased their kicking, screaming, and throwing, took their places at the table and began pouring tea like children trained at the finest etiquette school.

Lucy eased into a seat reserved for her across from Uncle Teddy. "What angels. You really have a way with the children, Celia," Uncle Teddy praised Celia in relief.

"You just have to use the right tone with them," she giggled.

"Mr. Sampson, what is it that you ship?" Lucy opened the small talk.

"Oh no, no shipping talk. I thought we could talk about the latest fashions in bonnets. I hear that ruffles are all the rage in France now," Celia quipped as she delicately picked at her lemon cake.

Lucy pondered her cake, poking at it with her fork as she plotted how to broach the subject of Shiloh. *How will I free a slave?* As if in answer to her quandary, the boy in question entered the room, visibly concentrating on not dropping the tray loaded with another pot of tea.

"That can go right here Shiloh." Uncle Teddy pointed to the empty spot on the table to his left. Shiloh carefully placed the tray on the table and, without looking at anyone, backed away a few paces and waited for the next command with his arms positioned stiffly at his sides. "That will be all Shiloh. You may return to the shop and finish sweeping the store room." Uncle Teddy took a sip of his tea and turned his attention to Lucy, as Shiloh slid out of the room silently.

"Now, Miss…"

"Lucy Cormac."

"Yes, Miss Cormac. How do you know our Celia?"

"We sailed on the *Queen Mary* together from…"

"Oh I heard, unfortunate business that. Pirates and all. Such horrid people. It must have been awful for you girls. These renegades are such a scourge to my business…"

For the next hour, Lucy listened to talk of the despicable behaviors of pirates, the beauty of the new dresses coming out of Paris, and the trials of training slaves in the appropriate ways of serving food. When there was not a drop of tea left, Uncle Teddy graciously stated, "Miss Cormac, you've been a delight. You must come back. Anything for a friend of our Celia."

"Actually, sir, I do have a favor. Might I speak with you privately?"

"Certainly, my dear. Right this way to my study."

Celia grimaced and whined under her breath at this need for a private word, but Lucy paid no mind and followed Uncle Teddy into the study. Uncle Teddy took a pipe out of his pocket, "Do you mind?"

"No, not at all sir."

The gentleman lit his pipe. "Wonderful, Celia's not fond of the pipe. So what can I do for you?"

"Well sir, you see, I am about to travel to the Carolinas to find my grandfather. He's my only living relative. I have my lady's maid Gracie, but I need another servant to help with my luggage. And from what I've heard of slave auctions, I just can't see going."

"Oh no, you mustn't. It's no place for a lady," he answered in horror to the idea.

"No, I can see that. What I'm asking..." She hesitated and dropped her eyes, "Sir, could I buy the little house boy who served us tea earlier?" She rapidly continued, "I wouldn't ask, but I think I should have some sort of male escort. I have no one else to ask for help."

Uncle Teddy took the pipe out of his mouth and ran his hand over his shiny head. "Yes, yes, I see your problem. And you shouldn't travel alone. Most definitely not. Although it would be hard to part with Shiloh. He is finally trained in the art of tea serving. It took years, let me tell you."

"Oh I know it's a lot to ask, never mind, it's just too much." Lucy covered her face with her hand and eked out a few tears. "I just feel so helpless. It's so hard being an orphan and a girl with no one to take care of me." Apparently Lucy was a pretty good actress.

Uncle Teddy patted Lucy on the shoulder. "Don't cry dear. If my Celia was in trouble I should hope that someone would come to her aid. I would be happy to give you Shiloh."

Lucy cried harder. "Thank you sir. Thank you so much." She took from her pocket the bag of coins Sebastian had just given her for shopping. "Here sir, this should pay for your loss."

"I cannot accept your money."

"I insist. You have been too kind already. You are a business man, please take it." Lucy placed the bag in Uncle Teddy's hand. "You have made me so happy, and I will never forget your kindness."

"You are welcome my dear. Never hesitate to ask me for anything. Now come, I'm sure you wish to be on your way."

***

Lucy exited the house with a very confused Shiloh. He had just been instructed to follow this strange woman. It was difficult to extricate herself from the house with Celia trailing after her, frantically trying to get her to stay; behind Celia the flock had returned to yelling and hitting. Eventually, Lucy and Shiloh were on the street in front of the house. Upon seeing Lucy and Shiloh appear on the street, a door slammed, and Gracie shot up from the servants' quarters. She grabbed her brother from behind and began sobbing. This so startled the boy, who could not see his attacker, that he too began to cry.

"Shiloh, Shiloh," Gracie cried in between tears. "It's me; it's Gracie."

Shiloh turned around and looked, for the first time in four years, into the familiar face of his sister. This brought on true tears. Lucy turned away as the two siblings hugged and wept in reunion.

Chapter 28

Gracie excitedly chattered to her brother, four years worth of chattering, as they turned down an alley in the direction of the Rooster's Crow. She retold the sorrow of losing their mother, her escape from Martinique, and all of the adventures that had followed, up until the present moment.

Shiloh was on the shorter side, but his hands and feet looked too large for his body. They hinted at a larger body soon to come. He listened quietly to his sister and looked at her as if she were his own personal hero. His eyes had gone from dead and flat to bright and twinkling in the matter of a conversation. And then a dam broke inside and a seemingly endless flow of words spewed out of Shiloh. He'd kept so much inside for too many years, but no longer. "Mr. Sampson taught me to keep his books. I know my numbers now. He also taught me my letters. I can teach you to read now Gracie, if you want me to. I like to read books about people in distant lands. I even got to travel to the city of London with Mr. Sampson. Everything was so big, but the people were strange; when I walked down the street everyone stared at me.

And so many people. You could never imagine so many people Gracie. We should go together; then I can show you. Someday I want to go to France. I saw a picture of the King of France in one of my books, and…"

Lucy walked slightly behind the siblings, allowing them some long overdue privacy. She listened to the joy in both of their voices, smiling to herself over her friend's success. At least one of them had found the family that she had gone in search of. Her smile faded a little at this thought, realizing that, by leaving tonight, she would be giving up her search for her own family. But her mind turned to Sister Regina, Lafitte, and Gracie. And now there was Shiloh, a new addition to this odd group of misfits. A family of sorts. She'd be leaving them too to be with Sebastian.

Sebastian. She lingered over this name. The name brought with it the memory of his lips on hers, made her blush slightly. The memory burned in her brain, becoming more vivid as she remembered each detail—the feel of his skin, heat of his breath, smell of the sun on him, and pressure of his hands. She was anxious to return to him as the need to physically see and feel him became more urgent.

She was abruptly thrown from these pleasant musings with the appearance of a dark figure shrouded in shadow. The shadow laughed with blood chilling cruelty. The three friends stopped in their tracks. Lucy and Gracie stood aghast as the figure moved into the light, revealing the hideous visage of Bonny. An evil smirk contorted his face, and a sword flashed in his right hand, ready for attack.

"I see the darkie is still followin' ye aroun'. This'll be bettr' an I thought. I'll get ye both. I've been made a fool fer too long. I'll finally get me revenge on that slut of a wife." Bonny menacingly began to close the gap between himself and his prey.

"Gracie, take Shiloh and run!" Lucy pulled the dagger that Sebastian had given her for protection out of her pocket and aimed it at Bonny.

"I'm not leaving you Lucy!" Gracie too pulled out her own knife, pushing Shiloh behind her skirt. "We stand a better chance together." The two women stood side by side, facing the danger together.

"Don't dare talk about Anne that way. Her biggest mistake was marrying you, a mistake she seems to have remedied. If you want us, come and get us. Gracie and I aren't running."

With this taunt, Bonny flicked his weapon and slashed at Lucy's knife wielding arm, leaving a bloody gash. Lucy's arm slouched in pain, dropping the knife. In agony, she grabbed at the fresh wound, attempting to staunch the flow of blood.

"I'll take ye apart bit by bit gurl," Bonny snarled.

Gracie stepped in front of Lucy and began screaming at Bonny in French and then launched her knife at his chest, but seeing the attack coming, he veered to the right enough that the knife sank into his left shoulder. He roared in rage as he pulled the dagger from his flesh and then raised his sword again, ready for his final attack.

"Stop. This is where it ends Bonny. You've haunted me and the people I love for too long. I'll finish what I started years ago, if you are brave enough."

The voice came from behind Bonny. Bonny turned to face his foe. He squinted, trying to recollect why the figure was so familiar. Age had changed it somewhat, but the demeanor had not changed in seventeen years. Bonny thought he was losing his mind for a second, as this female apparition from the past, dressed in the guise of a man, approached him with the fury of the devil. If his mind needed any more proof as to the identity of this ghost, it was confirmed when the personage dramatically ripped off the handkerchief tied round her head to reveal wild, red hair. It was much shorter than Bonny remembered, but it was still that same accursed color.

Lucy, through her pain, also saw the approach of the imperious figure through the shadows of the alley. The woman looked like someone Lucy had seen every day of her life, but she was so out of place in this alley with a sword strapped to her side. It couldn't be. She whispered in disbelief, "Mother Superior?"

"Anne Bonny. My little wife, why, I thought ye were dead."

"Unfortunately for you, I'm not. And don't ever call me wife you lazy leach of a bitch. I was out of my mind and desperate to leave my father's farm when I married you. But luckily I found Jack Rackham, a man a thousand times your worth, you worthless cur."

Lucy couldn't comprehend what was happening. *Anne Bonny? It can't be.*

"Anne, I'll take care of ye once an fer all, an then I'll take care a the gurl just fer kicks."

"You'll never have the chance you slug. I'll draw and quarter you before you touch a hair on her head." Anne drew a shiny sword from its sheath at her side. The sword looked at home in her hand, ready to slay anyone who might stand in her path. "Now shut your trap and let's get on with this. I've waited years to add to that scar."

Anne's sword flashed through the air as she leaped at Bonny, spryer than her years in a convent would deem possible. Bonny parried the blow, and then jabbed, hoping to find the heart, but Anne side stepped and cuffed Bonny on the back of his head with the butt of her weapon as he sailed past her. Bonny yelped but became more furious than ever, swinging his sword over his head, intent on letting the metal blade fall on Anne's red head.

Lucy gasped; her heart racing in fear for the woman she knew as Mother Superior. There was no way that a woman who had impersonated a nun for nearly twenty years could escape a fight with this creature Bonny unscathed. But Lucy hadn't known Anne Bonny, a woman born with fight in her, a weapon an extension of her arm. Anne was ready and anticipated Bonny's move; she ducked and lunged forward. The force of Anne's motion drove the cruel point of the polished blade into the middle of Bonny's chest with the learned accuracy of the adept swordswoman she was. Bonny froze with his sword held high in mid-air. Blood seeped from the wound in his chest. His eyes glazed over. A bloody drool oozed from his mouth. Then, his body collapsed onto the cobble-stoned street, a limp pile of flesh and clothing.

Anne spoke softly to no one in particular. "It's finally over my friends. Bonny is dead." Anne turned to Lucy, who was still clutching the wound on her arm. "You're bleeding badly." Anne tore the sleeve of her shirt off at the seam and then deftly wrapped Lucy's gash.

"It's not so bad. You have amazing timing Mother, or should I say, Anne?"

"Anne would be fine."

"And amazing aim with a sword," chimed in Gracie with due amazement. Lucy introduced Anne Bonny to Gracie and Shiloh.

"To take a man's life cannot be taken lightly. I would never have raised my sword to a man again, except for you Lucy." Anne gently touched the girl's cheek. "I pray that you never take a man's life. It tears a piece of your soul out each time. I have prayed for years to put my soul back together."

"How did you find us?"

"Sister Regina saw you and Gracie run off. When I got to the Rooster's Crow, and you still hadn't returned, I began to search the town. I know this town well, and I don't trust any of its inhabitants. You should never have gone off alone. I wasn't about to lose you, especially not to a man like James Bonny."

Lucy wrapped her arms around the woman who had cared for and protected her since birth. She winced with pain but wouldn't unlock her arms. "Are you truly the infamous Anne Bonny?" She could barely say the next words. "My mother?"

Anne stroked Lucy's dark hair. "Yes, I am Anne Bonny. This is true. I've lived in hiding since your birth. But there is much you don't know."

Chapter 29

Anne and Gracie maneuvered Bonny's body to a dark spot in the
alley and propped him up behind a stack of crates. By the time
they were done, Bonny just looked like another drunken lout,
sleeping off an afternoon's extravagance. Anne was confident that
no one would be missing him any time soon. And when someone
did eventually find him, they would assume that he finally pushed
one of his many enemies too far. No one would suspect that the
ghost of Anne Bonny had returned for revenge or, even more
absurdly, that a nun had struck the tyrant down. Frankly, all of
Nassau would be relieved that James Bonny was dead.

After stashing the body, Anne sent Gracie and Shiloh back
to the Rooster's Crow, for she wished to be alone with Lucy; there
was much to say. Now she was leading Lucy down a few cobbled
streets, outlined by dingy clapboard houses of various pastel
colors; sign boards marked the buildings as boarding houses,
public houses, or houses of prostitution. They continued, passing
through the residential section of town with its quaint cottages.
They trekked beyond where the houses stopped and a thick,

bristled grass grew in plenty. And still they trudged on. Anne noticed the Governor's white mansion and Fort Nassau, both perfectly situated to scan the seas. They began to climb a hill that loomed above the town at its feet. Upon reaching the summit, the two women stopped short in front of a faded gravestone. The sea shimmered with the afternoon sun, the town bustled below, and merchant ships set sail from port with precious goods. The occupant beneath the stone marker had silently watched all this activity day in and day out for seventeen years.

Anne Bonny stopped in front of the gravestone and bowed her head. She reached out her hand and stroked Lucy's dark hair. "I spent last night here, conversing with the dead. I needed to seek permission to speak of the past. And this is where you will find the answers you are seeking; although, I fear they are not the answers you want."

Lucy stepped away from the affectionate hand. "You are my mother, aren't you?"

"I have acted as your mother, protecting and sheltering you all these years, but..." She trailed off for a few moments, trying to force the words from her mouth. As if the action of speaking was too much, Anne fell to her knees in front of the grave. She placed her hand on the gravestone as if it were a dear friend's shoulder. Bitter tears streamed down her face, landed drop by drop on the grave. "This," she sputtered through the tears, "is where you will find your mother. She has slept here, watching the seas since your birth."

Lucy was dumb founded. She had been so sure that her mother was still alive, that one day she would meet this woman who meant so much to her. She looked at the headstone. "It can't be. She can't be dead."

"This is the last chapter of our story." Anne pulled the girl down beside her so that they were both at eye level with the inscription on the headstone— *Mary Read, Died 1721.*

Chapter 30

Fort Nassau Jail 1721

Mary and Anne had been in prison for months. Mary was growing very large. Anne was stuffing more and more rags and straw under her shirt to keep up with Mary's growth. Anne hadn't lied about being pregnant to the judge, but shortly thereafter, she had suffered a miscarriage. With the child went her last connection to Jack Rackham. Anne grieved over the loss for weeks and then turned her attention to Mary and keeping herself from the noose. She wasn't really sure what she would do when the child was actually supposed to appear, but for now, the rags were keeping the authorities at bay.

Mary was lethargic most days and sat listlessly in the corner of the dank cell, while Anne stroked her hair. At every stroke of her hand, Anne inwardly thought, this is not the ferocious woman whom I fought beside. Things were just not right. It was as if the life was being sucked from her by the growth in her belly.

However, it wasn't the belly, but the mind that was eating away at the expectant mother. Mary's thoughts centered round grief and regret during the long, dark hours stuck in jail. Grief for the death of Noah—a sweet man who never meant harm to a soul. Grief for the loss of Rackham and their other comrades. Regret that Noah would never meet his child. Regret for the lives she'd cut short. Regret that her innocent child would be born with the stigma of having two convicted pirates for parents—one hung for his crimes, the other rotting away in prison; their crimes would haunt the child's life. Regret that she and Anne were trapped in a dank prison cell, with no end in sight.

"Anne, I'd like to leave this place now. It smells funny, like sweaty boots and vomit. I think I may vomit." And then Mary did just that.

"My poor Mary. Who would have thought that a baby would…" She trailed off not realizing where her train of thought was taking her.

Mary looked straight into Anne's glistening eyes. "Would do me in?" she finished her friend's words. "Only for a woman of our kind would an innocent baby prove more lethal than a rapier to the gut. Noah would never believe it. I wish he were here with me now."

"You aren't done yet Mary. You're strong and young. You will see your child born; I promise."

"I may see her born, but I won't see her live."

"You are so sure that it will be a girl?"

"There is no doubt. Sometimes I hear her thoughts, and I dream about her every night. My bonny Anne, you must promise me that you will care for her as your own child and that she will never know her mother's infamous name or her mother's legacy. I want her to make her own path, free of my crimes. This life of piracy only ends in suffering and death. I want peace and security for this child. You must promise me this one last favor Anne."

Anne laid one hand on her friend's protruding belly and the other on her cold, pale cheek. "I will protect her as I know you would have done. She will never lack a mother and will be raised unaware of the past. She will have any future she wishes." With this promise given, Anne could feel a quick kick within Mary's womb in recognition of the vow.

"One last request, my bonny Anne. Name her Lucy. That was my grandmother's name; she was always good to me. And give her your surname, 'Cormac.' No one in the Caribbean has heard of a 'Cormac.' No one will know who she is or who her parents are with that name. And that will make Lucy a part of you too." Mary smiled weakly.

"I promise that little Lucy Cormac will want for nothing. Now please rest so that Lucy may actually meet her mother."

* * *

One month later in Nassau prison, on an unusually cold and rainy night, the cacophony of rain drops pelting the roof was

191

virtually silenced by a piercing scream of pain. Anne woke with a start. The body that she had been snuggled against in the night was now convulsing in agony.

"Mary, my sweet Mary, I'll call for a doctor. You'll be fine."

Anne crossed to the impenetrable iron bars of the cell and screamed at the top of her lungs, "Help! Call the doctor! Please, call the doctor! My sister is dying."

A scurry of activity in the prison began. Guards ran here and there calling for help; fellow inmates added to the chaos with their own yelling. Anne stayed close to her suffering friend, holding her hand and smoothing her brow, calming her after each convulsion of pain.

Not just one, but two doctors arrived, cloaked in black, with medical bags in hand. "How long has she been like this?" the shorter one asked.

"For about one hour now," Anne replied.

The doctors set to work— poking, prodding, and coaxing through the screams of the slowly fading mother. Mary's sweat soaked skin grew paler with each push.

"Anne, Anne," the suffering mother called.

"What is it my Mary?"

"I must write a letter. I must write to my daughter. Please, now, before I can't speak any longer."

The taller doctor, empathizing with the poor woman, went to find the jailer and returned with paper, quill, and ink. Through the moans and jolts of pain, Anne deciphered and scribbled Mary Read's last words.

Blood washed the filthy stone floor until finally a crying, slimy package emerged from the pain. And for this new life, Mary Read, the scourge of the Caribbean, gave her last breath.

Chapter 31

The good doctors turned away from the body splayed on the cold stone floor of the prison cell. The taller one with the misty eyes yelled out, "Guard, Guard!" A guard eventually appeared with straggly dark hair and a bayonet at the ready.

"This woman is dead. We're done here for now. We'll be back in a few hours with the undertaker to prepare the body."

Anne was positioned on the floor beside Mary's body, with her legs folded under her. A whimpering baby was nestled in her arms. Tears dripped off her cheeks onto the small face. She wondered how this sweet child could have left Mary so broken. "Your little Lucy is perfect, Mary."

The doctor continued talking to the guard through the bars of the cell. "We'll take the baby with us and find a home for her." The guard nodded in agreement. He had no interest in dealing with the child. He was relieved he wouldn't have to deal with the body of the dead woman either.

The other man of medicine stood above Anne and whispered a few words to her. She nodded in assent. He then reached out for the child. She paused, unable to relinquish the soft bundle. The doctor put his hand on Anne's red head and patted her gently. She caught his eye and the compassionate plea that lay within. Anne handed over the squirming baby reluctantly.

The doctors quietly departed and left Anne to mourn over Mary's body.

***

Anne sat by Mary, brushing the hair off her friend's forehead. She spoke to Mary all through the rest of the dark hours, remembering stories with her dearest friend. Anne couldn't believe that she was truly gone. Mary had too much life in her; she was always at the head of the fight, flying in the face of death. How could the mundane birthing of a baby be her undoing, a task that women were supposedly built for? As the first sign of daybreak streamed into the small barred window, Anne blurted through her sobs, "She's gone, Mary's dead!"

The guards appeared and glanced indifferently at the body on the floor and the sobbing woman at her side. "The undertaker's on the way." In the guards' minds Anne and Mary were convicted pirates; they deserved what they got.

On cue, the doctors appeared at the bars of the cell with an undertaker and a wooden coffin. One of the remorseless guards jangled his keys and unlocked the cell door to allow the visitors entry. All three men, Seamus, Silas, and Lafitte, looked sadly at the body and paid silent respect to Mary Read. Then they went to work with the plan that Silas and Seamus had arranged with Anne before their departure just hours earlier.

Using a nail meant for the coffin, Anne scrawled on the wall her last message to the Governor and her jailors. She then lovingly pulled a gold ring from Mary's lifeless finger. Anne kissed her friend's cold cheek one last time and then stepped into the open coffin and lay down. Silas and Lafitte placed the lid over Anne and firmly nailed it down. Seamus settled Mary in a corner of the cell, stroked her face, and whispered his goodbyes. He covered her corpse with a navy blanket that camouflaged the form amongst the dark space as he would have a child slumbering in her bed. Seamus then strew some old straw over Mary to further hide her from the guards' eyes. The three men each took hold of the coffin and made to exit the cell. They gave a last glance at the beloved form in the corner and then hastily departed.

Outside the prison walls, the pelting rain of the night before had subsided to a light drizzle and a dense fog. The air was heavy with moisture as the men hefted the coffin onto a waiting horse drawn cart. Silas and Seamus hopped in the back, on either side of the coffin. Lafitte climbed up on the box and took the reins. He coaxed the horse to a trot, and the cart and crew jostled out of the prison yard and back into the town proper through the mask of fog. The cart never halted until it reached the Rooster's Crow.

The compatriots set the coffin carefully on the floor inside the pub and pried the lid off. The "undertaker" proffered his hand to an anxious Anne and helped pull her up. "Thank you Lafitte," she said. Anne hugged him and then hugged Dr. Silas and Dr. Seamus in turn.

Lafitte pulled a bottle of rum from behind the bar, along with four glasses. He poured the brown liquid and handed a tumbler full to each of his comrades. "To Mary Read, the scourge of the high seas," Lafitte sang out. They each raised a glass and quaffed the rum.

A young woman emerged from the upper rooms of the inn. Cuddled in her arms was Mary's baby. Anne ran to her and scooped up the child.

"Hello sweet Lucy," she cooed. "I'll take you away, and no one will ever find either of us again."

Lafitte suggested that Anne steal away to Martinique, to the convent where his sister had been a resident for several years. Sister Regina could help Anne care for little Lucy, as Anne wasn't exactly the maternal type. By night fall, Anne and Lucy were safely smuggled out of New Providence.

***

Meanwhile, the prison guards were perplexed to find a body hidden in the corner of the cell, the message, *Your prison walls couldn't hold my spirit. –Anne Bonny*, scribbled on the wall, and no Anne Bonny anywhere in sight. The guards buried the body on the hill overlooking the prison and marked the grave with the inscription *Mary Read, Died 1721.*

Anne was able to slip out of New Providence with Mary's daughter before any real search began for the escapee. Rumors instantly sprang up in New Providence surrounding the disappearance of the infamous duo. Some said Mary Read died of a fever, her baby dying with her; others believed both she and Anne had escaped. Some believed Anne Bonny's father procured her release with his vast fortune. Silas, Seamus, and Lafitte added to these rumors with reports that Anne was sighted back in the Carolinas with her father or that they heard she was living on an uninhabited island with her child. More rumors sprang from the originals. No one actually knew if there was a child or if either of the women had actually been pregnant. And certainly, no one ever suspected that one of the most infamous women of the Golden Age of Piracy was safely hidden away in a convent with the daughter of Mary Read.

Chapter 32

"So that is the story, the whole story of the legends of Anne Bonny and Mary Read, my dear. I am sorry that you never knew the truth and that I was the one who kept it from you, but I was only doing what your mother asked. She wanted you to be free of the past and any mistakes she had made. She meant the best for you. She loved you even before she met you." Anne held Lucy by the gravesite of Mary Read as they both mourned for things lost.

"So this Noah Harwood, the one she fought the duel for, was my father?" Lucy confirmed softly.

Anne nodded, "He didn't belong on a pirate ship. He wasn't much of a fighter, but he was an excellent shipwright. He would have been better suited to a quiet, domestic life. I think he and Mary would have left the crew and settled somewhere out of the way...if we hadn't been captured. Piracy isn't exactly conducive to mothering; Mary couldn't very well have had a baby sucking on her teat while thrusting the fear of God into the heart of the enemy." Mother Superior paused. "They would have given you a good life. Mary's last thoughts were of you and the life you would lead. She made me promise to keep her identity hidden from you so that you could have a quiet life, a life free of prejudice. She didn't want you to have to live with the shame of the crimes she committed. I promised that I would protect you, which meant keeping the subject of your birth a mystery. For that I am sorry. It was a necessary evil." Anne apologetically patted Lucy's hand. They resumed staring at the name engraved on the headstone as if they expected it to come to life right in front of them.

Lucy's eyes dropped. The golden glint of her ring caught her attention. "Wait, what about my ring? If it's not from Captain Rackham to you, then where did it come from?"

Anne reached out and touched the ring. "This *was* my ring, but not from Jack. Mary gave it to me. The 'R' stands for..."

"Read," Lucy finished in understanding.

"Yes, I wanted you to have something connected to Mary. I gave her a matching ring." Anne pulled a chain from where it had been concealed beneath her blouse. Attached to the chain was a nearly identical golden ring. It only differed from Lucy's in the inscription. The face was engraved with an elegant "*M*." The inside read, *Always, my sister - B.*

Anne took the ring off the chain and rolled it over in her hands. "We were sisters. We honored that bond by exchanging these rings after our first battle together. I loved Mary like no other in my life. I took this ring from her before I escaped from the prison cell. I wanted a keepsake of hers, and I couldn't bear to think that a guard might steal it from her body. I've wanted to return it to her for many years now."

With misty eyes and unspeakable pain in her chest, Anne dug a small hole in the dirt right beneath the worn headstone. She placed the ring in the hole and then covered it over again. "Always, Mary, always."

Chapter 33

Anne and Lucy sat in silence by the grave for what seemed like ages. They couldn't pull themselves away. And then Lucy noticed the day turning to night. She realized Sebastian would be leaving in just a few hours.

"Anne, I need to get back. Sebastian must leave with his crew by midnight, and I'm going with him."

"So you plan to follow Sebastian and become a pirate?" her mood quickly changed to scorn.

"I'm an orphan and the daughter of a pirate. Where else do I belong but on a pirate ship?"

"After all you've learned, sitting here by the grave of your mother; how dare you choose the life that Mary wanted to protect you from. How could you do this to her? To me?" The woman she knew as Mother Superior spoke with a vehemence that Lucy didn't recognize. "Silas, Seamus, Lafitte, Sister Regina, and I have spent nearly two decades trying to protect you Lucy. And you would throw all of that love and commitment away for some man that you just met? You'd risk your life to be with him?"

Lucy had been sitting in silent shock at Anne's fury. But now she was seething with her own vehemence. "You say that you have been protecting me all these years Mother? What you've done is lied to me for seventeen years in order to control where and how I live, and then you tell me the truth about my existence as the only means to continue to manipulate me. You only revealed the truth because, for the first time, I acted against your wishes. And you dare to speak against Sebastian? He was the one who rescued both Gracie and me from prison, risking arrest to save us. So don't you dare speak against him. When I'm with Sebastian, I feel that I finally belong to a family." Lucy's fury began to wane and she fell silent for a few seconds. She glared at Anne.

Mother Superior glared back. She was hurt by what Lucy had said, but she was oddly comforted by it as well. For the first time in many years she felt like Mary Read was present again. Lucy had been right when she said she had never fought against Mother Superior. She secretly hoped that Lucy would put up a fight every once in a while; just a flicker of the stubborn mother and Anne would have felt her friend still lived. Now it seemed that Mary had been resurrected right in front of her eyes.

"You can't control me any longer. I'm not Mary, and I'm not you. I have my own destiny, and it lies with Sebastian."

Lucy pulled a blue ribbon from her hair and picked an orange poppy at her feet. Tying the ribbon around the stem, she lovingly placed it on the headstone and left Anne seated by the grave.

Chapter 34

Sebastian was nervously pacing in front of the Rooster's Crow as the hours stretched on and still no sign of Lucy. Upon finally spotting a gloomy Lucy, Sebastian leaped into motion, rapidly shortening the distance between himself and the object of his affections.

"Thank God you've returned. Lucy, what happened to your arm?" he worried at the sight of the blood soaked bandage wrapped round Lucy's right forearm.

Lucy smiled, but with hesitation. Her heart lurched with the touch of Sebastian's thumb brushing her pink cheek. "We ran into an old friend. Bonny. He wasn't too happy to see us though. If it weren't for Anne, I don't think I would have returned to you at all."

"Anne, as in Anne Bonny?"

"Yes, I finally found her. Turns out she has been with me since I was born, but not my mother." Lucy then proceeded to tell Sebastian all that had occurred since they had parted hours earlier, up until her falling out with Anne at the gravesite. Sebastian listened to the events, bouncing from outrage to concern to sympathy, as the circumstances dictated. After recounting all that she had learned, Lucy could only hold tight to Sebastian to steady herself. He was solid and real. She felt safe and secure within his arms. She just wanted to stay in that cocoon forever, but she knew it wasn't possible.

"I was afraid I'd have to leave without you. My ship sets sail in less than an hour. We have to leave shortly or Father, the Right Honorable Governor, will not hesitate to haul me and my entire crew to the gallows."

"Yes, of course. I just need to say goodbye to the others, and then we will depart." She released herself from the safe cocoon with a deep sigh. Gripping Sebastian's hand, she entered the tavern.

Lucy was greeted with relief and concern by Sister Regina, Silas, Seamus, Lafitte, and Gracie. The majority of those gathered in the room were most relieved that there were no longer secrets concerning Lucy's parentage.

Lucy noticed that Gracie had a glow about her that had not existed before finding her brother. The deep sorrow that permeated her being seemed to have lifted. Shiloh was sleeping upstairs at the moment, his first soft bed in thirteen years. Lucy took the opportunity to speak with Gracie about all that had transpired recently. After gaining a full grasp of all the events from the arrest to Mary's death, Gracie solicited her own burning question. "How did you two avoid the noose?" She was pointing at Silas and Seamus. "How were you able to doctor Anne and Mary?"

Seamus and Silas exchanged cowed looks. "We weren't captured with the rest of the crew," Seamus mumbled.

"We were so drunk that day that we fell overboard just before the soldiers attacked," Silas continued. "Hitting the water sobered us enough that we were able to swim to shore. We were anchored in a cove, and the shore was fairly close. We hid behind a rocky outcropping, listening to the rapport of gun fire and the clash of swords. We didn't move until the soldiers left."

"We've lived in shame ever since. We ran away like cowards as our friends were arrested," Seamus chimed in again. "The only good that came of it was we were able to offer our services as doctors when Anne and Mary announced they were pregnant. The judge needed confirmation. "

Silas added clarification, "We were in the courthouse the day Rackham's crew was sentenced. When we offered our medical skills, the judge jumped at the idea. There aren't many doctors on New Providence to begin with; fewer still that want anything to do with pirates. We became Anne and Mary's court appointed doctors and had complete access to them both while they were imprisoned. We did what we could for them. In the end, it allowed us to help Anne escape. For that, I am thankful for our cowardly acts."

They both hung their heads in shame and waited for the party to condemn them for cowardice.

"Thank you," Lucy whispered.

"For what my dear?" Silas questioned.

"You brought me into this world. You tried to save my mother, and if it weren't for you, Anne's miscarriage would have been found out, and she would have been put to the noose. You saved our lives."

"She's right, you kept us alive." Anne Bonny had appeared in the doorway. Anne was staring at Lucy, hoping for reconciliation. Lucy avoided her eyes, and a profound silence descended on the party. It seemed to last for hours. No one seemed willing to be the first to break the mood. Finally, Lafitte breached the silence. "There is one more piece to the story Lucy. *Cherie Rouge?*" he looked to Anne to be sure he was doing the right thing. She nodded her consent and smiled mildly at the old, familiar moniker. "Your mother wanted to be sure that you were taken care of. There is a box, upstairs, that has been in my care until the right time."

Lucy perked up at this latest tidbit. "She left me something?" She played with the ring on her finger, her one treasured heirloom. Sebastian lightly pulled at the skirt of Lucy's dress. "Come; let us see what this treasure is."

"This way," Lafitte urged. He led the party upstairs to a small space that looked like a storage room, as it was packed with old dusty chairs, crates of bottles, piles of rags, and so on. There was one window in the tiny room, opposite the door. The last beams of sunlight streamed in, illuminating the dust hanging in the air. Lafitte walked to the window. The windowsill was deep and wide, big enough for a person to sit comfortably and watch village life below. Lafitte began to pull and prod the wooden sill. It started to shift slightly; eventually, he pulled the entire top off, revealing a secret chamber.

Lafitte motioned Lucy forward. "This is your legacy my dear. Anne and Mary kept their most valuable possessions here, out of sight from the rabble they associated with. Sorry to those I may offend." He looked to Silas and Seamus in amends for his words.

"None taken," Seamus assured.

Lucy moved to the window, curious as to the contents. There in the chamber lay a box, not a small box, but one that took up the entire interior of the windowsill. It wasn't spectacular in any way, only a simple wooden box. Lafitte placed his hands on either side and, with a bit of muscular effort, yanked the mysterious object out of the windowsill.

"This is causing a bit of perspiration. It's as heavy as it looks," Lafitte complained. Silas took the hint and leaned in to help heft the box to the floor.

"It's yours to open, my dear," Lafitte nudged Lucy forward. "I didn't pull it out just so you could stare at it," he coaxed the motionless heiress. Sebastian placed his warm hand on the small of her back and pushed her gently towards the box.

"You're keeping us all in suspense. There is nothing we pirates like more than a box of treasure. You can open it, go ahead Lucy," Sebastian urged, first mockingly and then with sincerity and warmth.

Lucy bent down hesitantly, sliding her hand along the top and then, with decision, lifted the lid. Lucy gasped; it was like nothing she could have ever imagined. Seven pairs of eyes scanned the bank notes, gold coins, and various colors of jewels in awe.

"This was the best of the loot Mary, Rackham, and I ever took, and it is all left to you," Anne explained.

Lucy was overwhelmed with this treasure trove, but she was most intrigued by a letter that lay on top of the loot. Her heart raced as she gingerly touched the envelope with the words, *To My Lucy*. She picked it up and opened the letter along the crease. Lucy gazed at the lovely hand writing and took in the words silently, the last and only words from her mother.

My Dear Lucy,

I am very sorry to have never met you. There are many things that have been kept from you, most especially my identity and that of your father's, but I didn't want my past to haunt your future. The only consolation to the mystery of your parentage I can offer is this chest—all my worldly wealth I leave to you. I want you to be free, free of my mistakes and free of the limitations life can sometimes offer to a woman. Don't settle, but find your own path. Be happy and know that I always will love you.

Your Mother

Lucy read the words several times over before pressing the precious note to her bosom.

"Mary dictated this note to me just before she died. The plan was for Lafitte to send the note and the chest anonymously to the convent on your eighteenth birthday. You would then have had the ability to go and do whatever you wanted," Anne explained. "But now it's all yours to do with as you wish."

"To do with as I wish," Lucy repeated in a daze. She was trying desperately to make sense of the letter and this unexpected inheritance. She could do anything she wanted now. Lucy was confronted with the vastness of opportunity, an overwhelming position to face and one that can be more burdensome than limitation. *What does one do when given the chance to do or go anywhere they please?* "If you all would excuse us, I'd like to speak with Sebastian alone."

Assenting to her wishes, Anne, Silas, Seamus, Lafitte, Gracie, and Sister Regina left the couple alone.

Chapter 35

Lucy was still holding the precious note in her hands, memorizing
each word. Her mother had come back from the grave to offer her
advice. She knew she couldn't disappoint Mary's last wishes. Her
mother's one wish was that Lucy not follow in her footsteps, that
she be free to decide her own fate. Seeing Mary's last wishes,
Lucy finally understood the sacrifice and hardship that Mary,
Anne, Seamus, Silas, Lafitte, and Sister Regina had all endured for
her happiness, to keep her safe—safe from the world and safe from
the truth. She couldn't betray that sacrifice and love.

"Sebastian…," she trailed off, gulping back tears.

"You aren't coming with me," Sebastian whispered, hoping
what he knew in his heart wasn't true but somewhat relieved that
Lucy wasn't condemning herself to a life of constant danger.

"I can't." Lucy looked up into his eyes. "My mother died
wishing for me to have a different life than hers, and Anne hid
herself away for years to protect me. I can't let their sacrifices be
in vain. I have the ability to live as I choose, and a life of piracy is
not my choice, even though it means leaving you."

Sebastian pressed Lucy to him, and stroked her dark tresses. "I won't go. I'll stay with you."

Lucy gently slid her hand down the sinews of Sebastian's arm, entwining her fingers with his. She brought his hand to her face and softly brushed the palm of his hand with her lips. "No, Sebastian. You need to go with your ship now. I need to find my own path; I can't do that with you. You can't stay here without endangering your life, and I can't just leave Gracie, Shiloh, Anne, and Sister Regina behind. I'm so sorry my love."

"My love?" Sebastian questioned.

"Yes." With silent ceremony she slid her mother's ring onto the little finger of Sebastian's left hand. Lucy softly kissed the ring and then raised her deep brown eyes to Sebastian's quiet face, memorizing every facial feature. Looking into those sorrowful eyes he adored so much, Sebastian couldn't help but clasp Lucy to him for the last time and kiss her with the force of every ounce of his being. He let her shaking hand fall and then turned quickly, leaving Lucy standing like a statue as he disappeared from the room.

***

Lucy slowly descended the stairs into the lower level of the inn and threw herself into the waiting arms of Sister Regina. Sister held her tightly and stroked Lucy's hair as the distraught girl sobbed on her shoulder. The past couple of days had been a blur of discovery and loss. The loss of Sebastian was the final straw. Lucy cried as she hadn't since she was five and a beloved doll had been swept out to sea while she was collecting shells.

Eventually, the sorrow began to subside. Lafitte brought her a shot of his best whiskey, Gracie made her a plate of mashed peas and stewed chicken, and Anne administered to the bleeding gash on her arm. Shiloh had reemerged from his nap and was now happily gorging on chicken. She joined the lad at his table and half-heartedly nibbled on her repast, surrounded by a whole group of people attempting to console her.

Lucy looked from one expectant face to the next, marveling at the fact that she had found a family, an unusual one to be sure—made up of ex-pirates, inn owners, ex-slaves, and nuns—but a family nonetheless. This scene brought her a sense of peace; it had been family that she had been seeking all along, for her entire life. It had only appeared in an unorthodox form, which didn't decrease the bonds they all shared in any respect. But there were two people missing.

"Where are Silas and Seamus? They didn't leave already, without saying goodbye?" Lucy was suddenly saddened again.

Anne handed her a note. "They aren't fond of goodbyes. It makes them too sentimental and weepy, but they left this for you."

Lucy perused the note from the two eccentric "uncles" she had inherited in the last couple of weeks.

Our Dearest Lucy,

We don't believe in goodbyes, for nothing is finite, especially not time. What are considered endings are more often beginnings. Endings are limiting, but beginnings present endless opportunities. Be proud that you are your mother's daughter, but even prouder to be Lucy Cormac. Our paths shall meet again in our crisscrossing through time.

Silas and Seamus

Lucy smiled to herself upon reading these words that could only have been scribed by the likes of Silas and Seamus. Their wise words began to seep into her brain, sparking the glimmer of an idea. Lucy re-read the epistle to the gathering, from which a conversation began and the seeds of Lucy's idea started to take root. Lucy had a fortune at the ready; she just needed a worthy purpose, a purpose that would honor her parents and herself. It was also imperative to keep this new found family of hers together. Whatever the future held for Lucy, it would include Gracie, Sister Regina, Lafitte, Shiloh, and Anne Bonny.

Afterward

7 Months Later

Sebastian received a mysterious message from Lafitte seven months after parting from Lucy. Every day the memory of her swirled in his head; he was constantly distracted with wondering where she was and what she was doing. His life at sea was not nearly as satisfying as it once had been. But the note that reached him several days earlier brought him a new sense of hope and to the docks of St. John.

The island of St. John was a quiet island reserved for sugar plantations, mostly inhabited by slaves. The port only had a few ships docked in it and a few sailors loading crates of sugar into the hulls. It was an out of the way island, perfect for avoiding the authorities.

Sebastian wandered along the docks until he was positioned in front of the ship he had been summoned to. Automatically, he rubbed the ring on his left pinky with his thumb, a habit he had formed since the ring had been placed on his finger months earlier. Whenever the thought of Lucy entered his conscious or

217

subconscious mind he felt for the ring as if it were still attached to her hand. Due to the frequency of these thoughts of his beloved, the ring's band had grown as smooth as glass.

He stared up at the bow of the ship, shielding his eyes from the glare of the sun. His eyes came to rest on a figure with dark hair pulled back from her face, a navy blue linen shirt, and loose fitting, crimson red pants. The figure was waving to him. He squinted and drew closer. The figure came into focus. *Lucy!* Sebastian made his way up the gang plank, not daring to take his eyes from the woman for a second for fear that it was an apparition. Lucy met him at the top of the gang plank and threw herself into his arms. He in return crushed her to him.

"We've been waiting for you. Another few hours and we would have had to set sail without you," Lucy whispered into his chest.

Sebastian soaked in the smell of Lucy and nuzzled her neck, quietly breathing, "I missed you."

"That's good because I have a proposition for you Sebastian. Would you please follow me to my chambers?" Lucy slowly pulled away from Sebastian and entwined her fingers in his, leading him across the deck and through a door into a grand room at the stern of the ship. The quarters were decorated with a desk that faced towards a stained glass window looking out to sea, a four poster bed, ornate rugs covering the floor, paintings of landscapes on the walls, and a settee beside a small table set with afternoon tea. It was actually very livable; both homey and lavish at the same time. It was the most well decorated chamber Sebastian had ever encountered on a ship. Lucy led Sebastian to the window box that looked directly out the stern of the vessel. Lucy was about to leave a seated Sebastian on the window box and prepare the tea when he gently pulled her toward him until she was neatly nestled on his lap, wrapped in his arms.

"So, tell me love, why do you have a ship, and why have I been summoned?" Sebastian asked in between soft kisses.

"I want you to be the captain of this ship," she whispered.

Sebastian halted his lips and looked at her with concern and confusion. "You aren't going to become a pirate are you?"

"Yes and no." Sebastian arched his eyebrows at her. She spoke hastily before he could comment again. "I decided to use my inheritance to buy the freedom of slaves and take them to colonies where they may live out a free existence. Those who want may stay and work on the *MaryAnne* for a wage. You see, we'll also be a merchant vessel, transporting goods between the colonies."

"The *MaryAnne?*"

"Yes, that's what I named the ship. To honor the woman that gave birth to me and the woman that raised me, my mothers."

"And you want me to be the captain of this endeavor?"

"No, you are the captain of the ship. I can't do it. I'll probably spend the first couple of weeks bent over the side of the rail. But Gracie and I are the captains of the endeavor. Gracie will use her contacts to select the people, and I am the money."

Sebastian ran his hand through his unkempt, sun-bleached locks, trying to absorb the proposition that Lucy was embarking on. All the problems he saw with this venture and dangers they might encounter swarmed in his head. "I assume you already know what a difficult mission this will be. People are not going to willingly allow you to take their slaves."

"And that is why I have assembled a crew of some of the most hardened scalawags of the sea. It can't be any more dangerous than piracy?" Lucy quickly went on, "I have also employed several lawyers and am making contacts with those involved with abolition. No, it won't be easy, but I don't think a life of ease runs in either of our veins."

"What about my own crew and ship? Am I to just leave them?"

Lucy smiled bashfully. "Anne has told me that the Golden Age of Piracy is dead. That piracy is even more dangerous now than it was in her day. More difficult for those in your profession."

Sebastian looked at her curiously, wondering where this was going. Lucy continued on hastily, nervously playing with Sebastian's collar. "I could use another ship in my fleet. I already

220

have too many shipments to make. How would your crew feel about living within the law? They would be well compensated."

Sebastian scratched his scruffy chin. "I can't make the decision for the crew. We'll have to put it to a vote, and any man who wants no part in your scheme will be free to leave. But you have my blessing."

Lucy kissed him quickly in her excitement. "You'll have the command of two vessels. You'll be Admiral Strongbow. Maybe you and your father will be able to come to an agreement now that you will be a legitimate businessman."

"Let's not get ahead of ourselves. It's not for the welfare of my crew or my father that I agree to your wild scheme. Where you go Lucy, I go. And with this ring," Sebastian slipped Anne's ring from his finger and placed it back on the finger of its rightful owner, "I bind myself to you." He gently placed his hands on either side of the beautiful face and pressed his lips to hers. Time slipped away as the pair reveled in their reunion and spoke of their plans for the future, until a knock at the chamber door roused them from their happy bubble.

"Lucy, ahem, Lucy!"

It was Gracie trying to get her attention.

"We are loaded and ready to depart whenever you're ready."

Lucy and Sebastian were loath to be parted from the moment, but preparations needed to be made. Sebastian returned to the *Peril*. Most of the crew was happy to follow their captain into a new adventure. As long as they were paid and permitted to maintain their own shipboard rules, it made no difference which side of the law they fell on. Most of them were fully aware that the era of piracy in the Caribbean was rapidly disappearing; they would have to adapt or disappear.

With the acquisition of the *Peril*, Sebastian returned to Lucy and the *MaryAnne*.

"Ok, captain, the ship is yours," Lucy commanded happily.

"I've made arrangements to meet the *Peril* on the open sea, just beyond the reef around the island. Silas will become the captain and Seamus the quartermaster, since the former quartermaster wants nothing to do with your endeavor."

Sebastian took his place at the helm of the ship and began making the commands to ready the *MaryAnne* to set sail. Gracie went to reel in the anchor with Shiloh at her side. Sister Anne, as she wanted to be known to maintain the hidden identity of Anne Bonny, was instructing a group of newly freed men and women in the art of letting fly the main sail.

Anne refused to leave Lucy to her own devices. She wasn't about to abandon her promise to keep Lucy safe; she was also secretly thrilled to return to a life at sea. It's where she truly felt at home.

Sister Regina, however, returned to the convent on Martinique where she would take over the duties of the Mother Superior. Lucy wanted Sister Regina to join her band of renegades, but Sister was adamant that her path was to serve God. She had spent more than half her life in the quiet of the convent; she was happy there. Lucy bid her a tearful goodbye several months earlier with the promise of an aggressive correspondence.

Lucy looked on with a full heart at all the activity and marveled at the family that had sprung up around her. She was thrilled that Silas and Seamus would be part of her plan. They would certainly need well trained doctors to administer to those struck down by the hardships of life at sea. Lafitte would remain her contact on land, a place for them to dock and resupply. She smiled at Sebastian, perfectly at home at the helm of the ship. Surrounded by these people, her family, with her dreams for the future, and the memories of her parents, Lucy finally felt as though she'd found the place where she belonged in the world. The sea and the need for adventure that lay in her bones beckoned; the horizon stretched in front of her, full of endless possibilities.

Author's Note:

Fact behind the Fiction

Though I hate to admit it, Lucy Cormac is a fictional character. Anne Bonny and Mary Read were captured, along with their crew and put on trial in Spanish Town, Jamaica in 1720. Both women pled pregnancy, escaping the noose, but not imprisonment. Mary Read contracted an illness while in prison and died without having a child. It is unclear if she was ever pregnant. She died in April 1721 and was buried in Spanish Town. What became of Anne Bonny remains a historical mystery. She seems to have just disappeared from prison, whether or not with a child, no one knows. It is believed that she escaped from prison and returned to her father's plantation in the Carolinas or returned to the sea under another name or returned to the Carolinas and became the mother of numerous children. From the legend of Anne and Mary's supposed pregnancies spawned the idea of Lucy Cormac. What if Anne or Mary actually did have a baby; what would have happened to her, and what would it be like to be the daughter of pirate royalty? Lucy Cormac is my imagining of the legend.

Anne Bonny was born in Ireland, the illegitimate daughter of William Cormac and his servant. The family moved to Charles

Towne and lived well. Anne married James Bonny at an early age, against her father's wishes. The couple went to New Providence, but Anne quickly left Bonny for Captain Calico Jack Rackham after Bonny began selling information about pirates to the authorities.

Rackham was the quartermaster to the pirate Charles Vane, until the crew voted Vane out and named Rackham captain. He was known for his sense of style and creating the infamous Jolly Roger flag. After his crew's capture and trial, Rackham was hung and then placed in a cage for all to see his decomposing body on November 18, 1720 in Spanish Town, Jamaica.

Mary Read did live as a boy in her early life in order to receive financial assistance from her grandmother. She later joined the navy and married one of her fellow sailors. After he died, she arrived in the Caribbean and joined Rackham's crew. Anne and Mary became fast friends and notorious women of the high seas. Mary fell in love with a member of Rackham's crew and fought a duel to protect him; although, his name is unknown. Noah Harwood, however, was the name of one of the members of Rackham's crew that was tried and hung.

Woodes Rogers was a former English privateer who was sent to govern the notorious pirate den of New Providence in 1718. He succeeded in bringing an end to the Golden Age of Piracy and transforming the colony into a more civilized domain of the British realm. However, he did not have a son who was a pirate captain.

There are some sources that say Anne had a very good friend named Pierre who ran a house of ill repute. This is the basis for the character of Lafitte.

Sebastian, Simon, Silas, and Seamus unfortunately never existed, but they are based on those who chose a life of piracy. Gracie and her family too are fabrications, but representative of the thousands of nameless slaves that labored on the plantations of the French Caribbean.